COUNTESS
CARROTS

Books by Molly Costain Haycraft

Countess Carrots
The King's Daughters
My Lord Brother the Lion Heart
The Lady Royal
The Reluctant Queen
Too Near the Throne

COUNTESS CARROTS

by
Molly Costain Haycraft

J. B. LIPPINCOTT COMPANY
Philadelphia and New York

U.S. Library of Congress Cataloging in Publication Data

Haycraft, Molly (Costain) birth date
    Countess Carrots.
    I.   Title.
PZ4.H413Co   [PS3558.A8286]   813'.5'4   72–11773
ISBN–0–397–00963–1

To the Memory of
Lynn Carrick

1

I looked up into the small square of cloudy glass hanging high on the wall of the little retiring room, but although I stood on tiptoe all I could see of myself was the widow's coif that hid most of my Percy red hair and the drooping black veil that framed my thin shoulders. As I was alone, I made a disgusted grimace at the brown-eyed girl staring dimly back at me and turned away.

The chamber was cold on this cheerless February day, and I wondered how the other ladies here at Whitehall Palace kept warm in their luscious satin robes, draped artfully to display most of their bosoms. My black dress was long-sleeved, of course, and high-necked. But as I glanced down at the hateful garment, concealing the fifteen-year-old body of which I was rather proud, I remembered the horrible day two years earlier when I had had to kneel beside Harry, the stupid, vicious young Earl of Ogle, and hear the chaplain pronounce us man and wife. This sable gown, I decided, was a small price to pay for the privilege of being his widow.

Realizing suddenly that I had lingered longer in the retiring room than I should, I walked reluctantly out into the long, stone-floored corridor. Had the fog begun to lift at last? I turned into one of the deep window embrasures and pressed my face against the thick old glass. Was that flickering fuzzy light a lantern on the mast or prow of a boat down there on the Thames? Or was it a torch set on the palace parapet?

Whichever it was, I decided that the thick cloud curtain must be lighter than it had been when my grandmother and I left Northumberland House a few hours ago. We had proceeded in our chairs at a snail's pace, the world around us invisible and apparently deserted. More than once, however, our bearers had come to a jolting halt, warned by shouts from our footmen that another chair or coach was dangerously close.

Having no further excuse for peering out of the narrow window, I left the embrasure and continued on down the corridor. Before I had taken more than a step or two a sharp little bark, the scuttling patter of paws on the stones, and the sight of a small furry thing hurtling toward me made me pause again. I knelt and caught the panting dog in my arms: it was a spaniel, the King's favorite breed, white with ginger patches, reminding me vividly of my own dear Whiskers. I gathered the warm, squirming body closer, astonished that a cat and a dog should look so much alike.

As I raised it from the floor it gave my face a moist kiss, and I was smiling with delight when a deep voice startled me.

"Hold the rascal for me, my lady. He's given me a merry chase."

Glancing up, I saw a tall, richly dressed man striding toward me, his long heavy-featured face made strangely charming by a gentle look in his dark eyes and a warm smile on the large mouth under a thin black mustache. I gasped, almost dropped the dog, and managed, somehow, to sink down in my deepest court curtsy.

"Your Majesty!"

"Here, let me have him." One bony hand, partly hidden in a foam of creamy lace, took the spaniel out of my arms; the other raised me to my feet.

"Well," he said, his eyes running from the top of my widow's coif to the tips of my shoes, "Frisky has a habit of seeking out our prettiest ladies. But your face is new to me, my dear."

I felt the blood surge up into my cheeks but, frightened as I was, the question in his voice forced me to raise my head and answer him. "I'm—Elizabeth Ogle, sire. My lady grandmother brought me here today for the first time."

"Ah! Of course. Now I know." And taking my hand again, he drew me into the light. "The little Lady Ogle. Of course. So Lady Percy finally obeyed my order." He studied my gown and veil for a moment, pulling his mouth into a grim line. "But Lord Ogle died in 1679, well over a year ago. These robes seem hardly suitable in the circumstances, and for one so young!"

After a moment's silence, for I could think of nothing to say in reply, he shook his head understandingly.

"I suppose, having tried to keep you from Court with the excuse that you were still mourning a lad you saw only at the altar, your grandmother thought you must dress the part for me." He laughed shortly. "The Dowager Countess of Northumberland never does things by halves."

My telltale color, that curse of redheads, deepened even more and I stared at the floor, trying to evade his sharp, probing gaze. King Charles's assumption was only too true; I knew she had taken malicious pleasure in robing me thus.

"If his Majesty insists on having a widow at his Court,"

my grandmother said, after his second command arrived at Petworth, "he shall have one." And our sewing women worked through two nights making my weeds, burning a dozen working candles to their sockets. Indeed, I had never worn the somber, uncomfortable garments until today.

"But, my dear child, why are you here alone?"

The King looked up and down the endless corridor, empty now except for the guards standing at attention in a distant doorway. Then a smile again tugged at the corner of his full lips.

"Are you waiting for a—friend, perhaps? Some lucky young dog? Shall I—?" He made a move, as if to leave me.

"Oh, no, your Majesty!" I protested, so shocked that I could not keep my voice steady. "How could you think—? I wouldn't dare—" The very suggestion in his amused tones terrified me. "I slipped away from Lady Lucy Hay for a moment only. The—the air in Madame de Keroualle's salon was so heavy, and Lady Percy had been playing basset there for hours, and so many strangers kept coming in and out! Forgive me, sire, if I have done something very wrong," I faltered, "I'm new to the ways at Court." Then, not knowing what else to add, I blurted out the truth. "I'm shy."

As his black eyes met mine, I saw them grow even gentler than before, and he took my fingers in his for the third time. "But, of course"—he nodded—"and I'm frightening you. You are trembling. Has no one told you that everyone is shy here at first? Until they learn what an informal place my Court is, I mean. We're a sad lot, I'm afraid. Lady Percy, I know, deplores our free and easy ways."

While I stood there, motionless, he made a graceful leg, raised my hand to his lips and kissed it formally, then dropped it.

"If I say that your manners please me very much indeed, perhaps you will not be so shy again. Just say to yourself,

'King Charles finds me delightful to talk to and everything that is charming. And he should know, for he has a pretty taste in lovely ladies.' Which," he finished reflectively, "makes me a shockingly conceited fellow."

His eyes twinkled, and I realized suddenly why Lord Wilmot had dubbed him the "merry monarch." My timidity melted away, and I laughed aloud. "You have said enough, sire, to make me a shockingly conceited girl. But I think I should ask your permission to return to my grandmother and Lady Lucy. Neither of them saw me go, and I shall be scolded roundly."

"And so shall I," said the King, smiling warmly at me. "I seem to have lost both my Captain and my Principal Officer. And as I'm not supposed to take a step without them I shall suffer their most disapproving frowns when they find me here, as they will. Wait with me, and we'll let them escort us in full state to Madame Louise's apartments. Lady Percy cannot be too angry when I say I detained you."

With a long finger, he tipped my face up and studied it. "I see both your handsome father—you have Joscelyn's full Percy mouth—and your beautiful mother. She has these dark well-marked brows and the same large, wide-set brown eyes, if I'm not mistaken. But now, before we're interrupted, I want to ask you a question: Has Lady Percy told you that I would like you to be my little daughter-in-law?"

I looked back at him in bewilderment. How could I be his daughter-in-law? He and Queen Catherine had no sons—no children at all. Then his meaning reached me, and I tried to think which of his illegitimate sons might be the one he was talking about. I had heard that except for the Duke of Monmouth they were all small boys.

"No, sire," I replied, "but she tells me nothing—except, of course, what I must and must not do."

He nodded and flicked at the lace ruffle under his large

chin. "An imperious lady, your grandmother. Patterns her manners after those of another Elizabeth, the high and mighty Queen whose name she bears."

I almost smiled, for he was more right than he knew. My grandmother, Lady Elizabeth Percy, born a Howard and now the widow of the tenth Earl of Northumberland, was certainly more regal in her ways than the present Queen. "She does indeed," I said. "I am not even allowed to sit in her presence without her permission."

His black eyebrows rose almost to the edge of his wig. "What? But that marriage she hurried you into made you a countess, too—and *you*, after all, are the heiress to all the vast Percy fortune, not she!"

I shook my head. "I'm only her granddaughter: Lisa when she is affable, Elizabeth when she is angry."

His Majesty frowned and the smile left his eyes. "I was extremely distressed at the awkward way your young father's death left you situated," he told me. "You should be in your mother's care, not hers. Perhaps I should have interfered— I was tempted to, knowing Lady Percy—but not believing, as my grandfather did, that the King is above the law, I held my hand. However, I can and will stand your friend, and from now on I shall see that your guardian does not abuse her position of trust. *If* I can."

Before I could thank him his two royal ushers appeared from the nearest doorway and fell to their knees in front of him.

"Oh, there you are! I was beginning to wonder," said his Majesty, most unfairly, I thought. Catching me looking at him, he gave me a sly, knowing wink. "Well, on your feet, gentlemen, and lead us to the Duchess of Portsmouth's rooms. As we should not lose each other again, I will tell you now that I plan to make a short visit there and then be off to St. James's Park to sup with Madam Gwyn."

Without another word our small procession marched the length of the corridor, passed through the antechamber to Madame de Keroualle's withdrawing room, and paused at the door. The Captain stepped forward, holding his gold and ebony staff well in front of him, and announced the King.

Immediately behind him walked the second usher, armed with his silver and ebony staff; then King Charles, with me on one arm, Frisky still under the other. My legs were trembling a little with nervousness, and I kept my eyes on the floor until we were well inside the elaborately furnished chamber, lighted on this foggy afternoon by dozens of wax candles in heavily carved silver sconces and candelabra. Only then did I find the courage to search the bowing, kneeling, curtsying group for my grandmother.

I saw, from the manner in which the cards were scattered on the tables, that everyone had jumped up when the first usher entered. Madame Louise hurried forward to welcome the King. Over her head (covered with tight tiny curls from nape to forehead), my frightened eyes met my guardian's, which seemed to be jumping out of her face, her mouth—a cruel one, I always thought—was drawn into lines of horrified astonishment.

To my great relief, his Majesty did not abandon me. After replying briefly to his French mistress's babble of greeting, he led me directly across to my grandmother.

"I want to thank you, my dear Countess, for bringing Lady Ogle to Court as I suggested. If you have been missing her"—his tone could not have been more casual or his smile more gracious—"it is because we spent a short time making friends over the silken head of my naughty Frisky here." As he spoke he bent his cheek and rested it on the dog's floppy ear in an endearing, caressing way. "She caught him for me just outside one of the withdrawing rooms, and I would not allow her to return to your care until I had had the pleasure of a few moments' conversation. I must tell you how charming I find her, and how much I look forward to seeing her often here at Whitehall—or wherever my Court happens to be."

While my grandmother answered him in a stiff frigid voice, I moved quietly to my duenna, Lady Lucy Hay, and whispered my apologies for running away earlier. She tried to smile, but I could tell from the expression on her plain, almost chinless face that she knew the King's intervention would not save *her* from a severe scolding.

Poor Lady Lucy! My lot was a hard one, certainly, but I have always been eternally grateful that I do not stand in her shoes. Imagine being born the only daughter of the Earl of Carlisle and, at nearly sixty years of age, earning your keep by being at my grandmother's beck and call!

She has told me that when she was twelve her father died, leaving her penniless, and that her half brother, the new Earl, inherited debts of eighty thousand pounds with the title and not one unencumbered house or acre of land. In their lifetime, their father ran through a fortune of more than four hundred thousand pounds, apparently giving no thought to his children or their future.

But because Lady Lucy's mother was a Percy, my grandfather kindly took her into his household and always treated her with gentle courtesy. Although she has never said so, I am sure that her timid, scuttling ways and even her limp developed after his death, when he was no longer there to protect her from his wife's iron will and cutting tongue, the will and tongue that ruled us both.

An old friend drew Lady Lucy from my side a few minutes later and I remained where I was, watching the dazzling scene around me. The creamy shoulders and rounded bosoms of the ladies, only lightly veiled by their muslin chemisettes, the handsome coats and long, richly brocaded or embroidered waistcoats worn by the noblemen, their foaming lace cravats, tall gold-headed canes, heavily curled perukes—I sighed, feeling like a black crow caught in a flock of birds of Paradise. Realizing suddenly that I was standing in front of a scarlet and gold tallboy, an unusual piece of Chinese lacquer newly arrived from the East to grace the Duchess of Portsmouth's chamber, and that my weeds against its splendor must make me horribly conspicuous, I looked around for a quiet corner.

Before I could move, however, a stir at the far side of the salon halted me in my tracks. A nursemaid led a small boy to Madame Louise, and when the Frenchwoman took him to the King's side and the child held up his cheek for a kiss, I cannot say I was surprised. The likeness between the two was so great that I was sure they must be father and son.

I *was* surprised, though, to see his Majesty present him to my grandmother and, in response to something he said as he did so, to see her glare angrily and stiffen.

A nasty, unpleasant surmise flashed into my mind; I dismissed it, at first, as impossible, for the boy could not be more than six years old. Then I remembered King Charles saying that he wanted me for a daughter-in-law. As I fought a feeling of horror, the months rolled back to a day two years ago, a day I had tried to forget.

I was in my own chamber at Petworth, looking out of a window while my dresser went to find another pair of hose. A moment later I was running swiftly down the steep stone staircase and into the courtyard where I had just seen a thin ferret-faced lad of about fifteen chase a small fluffy kitten up a magnolia tree.

He had a large stone in his hand, and as he raised his arm to throw it I reached him, clutched at him, and screamed, "Stop, stop, stop!"

He looked down at me, and his slack mouth fell open. No wonder he was surprised! I must have been a strange sight —a thin-faced fury with a cloud of red hair blowing loosely on the shoulders of an elaborate satin gown, dancing up and down with rage, my feet bare and pink on the cobbles.

"Beast—beast!" I pummeled him with one hand, then, letting go of his arm, I pushed him violently against the rough stone chapel wall. He must have been caught off guard by my attack, for he reeled back and dropped the stone. Almost before it reached the ground I had it, moved a pace away, and measured the distance between us.

"Now!" I took a careful aim, my eyes narrowed. "I'll teach you to persecute a poor little kitten!"

Before I could throw it a commanding voice rang out from the doorway.

"Elizabeth Percy! what in the world?" My grandmother, her plump, middle-aged body clad in a rich velvet robe, rushed between us, her skirt dragging over the stones. "Half dressed, your hair every which way—and *bare feet!*"

"He was stoning a cat, madam." I tried to excuse myself and hide the fear I always felt in her presence. "See, it's climbing down the magnolia tree." As I spoke the kitten, white and round, marked here and there with patches of fur as red as my hair, jumped to the ground and scampered to my side. I scooped it up and it nestled close to me, purring.

While I held it protectively, my grandmother, her large eyes even more protuberant than usual, stared at the gangling, ugly boy, still crouching against the wall.

"Disgusting!" she said. "Disgraceful! I'm ashamed of both of you. To find you, my lord Ogle, behaving like a hobbledehoy while your father is in the very act of signing your marriage papers! And as for you, Elizabeth, if this were not your wedding day I would, believe me, find it necessary to whip you. Now back to your dresser this instant. Tell her I want you ready for the ceremony before the clock strikes the half hour."

Less than an hour later, as I knelt beside my bridegroom, the young Earl of Ogle, I remember wondering desperately why someone had not saved me from this fate. My always absent mother, my powerful uncle, the Earl of Essex—or even our chaplain, John Price, who was standing before us and tying the hated knot—how could they allow it to happen to me? Until the words "I pronounce you man and wife" were uttered, I kept hoping that my mother would rush into the chapel to stop the grim ceremony.

But I became the Countess of Ogle; my husband, as was the custom in such an early union, was sent abroad before nightfall, to travel there until such a time as we might both be old enough to assume the responsibilities of marriage.

However much I have tried to forget that day, I often linger over the memory of the one less than eight months later when the letter reached us, informing us of his death; "premature decay" was the cause mentioned. What was "premature decay," I kept asking myself. Well, I know more about it now; Harry came from bad stock, and it was a shocking business to wed me to him. His sister went mad and so would he have done by now, had he lived. . . .

Surely, I told myself, my lady grandmother would not force me into another distasteful alliance, this time with an illegitimate boy less than half my age. But if the King insisted, what could she do? I was shuddering at the thought when an announcement at the chamber door put it out of my mind for the moment.

"The Lady Harvey," a lackey shouted over the hum of the conversation. "And the Count of Königsmark."

Lady Harvey was the sister of my stepfather, Ralph Montagu, and the few times our paths had crossed I had found her a most disagreeable and malicious woman. Deaf, and with a voice that sounded like the piercing scream of a parrot, she had a gift for irritating almost everyone.

But as I watched her enter, the stranger beside Lady Harvey made me forget all else, for he was by far the handsomest man I had ever seen. Almost head and shoulders taller than anyone else in the room, he was broad-shouldered and slim-legged; instead of wearing a stiffly curled wig, his own pale-gold hair swept down over the collar of his green velvet coat. A firmly modeled chin above the lace ruffle of his cravat belied any hint of effeminacy, as did the bold sapphire eyes set widely apart.

At first those eyes glanced around the assembled company idly. Then, over all the other heads, they met mine and I saw him start and take a step forward. He bent down and whispered in Lady Harvey's ear.

She looked across the chamber at me and waved a jeweled hand.

"Oh, that?" A loud laugh followed the equally loud words, and a hush fell over the room. "That's Countess Carrots. You must have heard of her, Carl—Ralph's step-daughter. My wealthy little niece!" And she laughed again. "She's maid, wife, and widow," she went on shrilly, "and only fifteen years old."

Realizing that everyone was staring at me, I raised my chin and blinked back a mist of tears. Countess Carrots— what a hateful name! How long had people been calling me that?

While I fought to regain my composure, I saw my tactless kinswoman present the tall stranger to King Charles. I could tell, from the King's manner, that this was no casual visitor to Whitehall, and I was still wondering who he might be when, to my horror, his Majesty, trailed by Lady Harvey, led the young man to where I was standing.

"My dear Lady Ogle," he said gaily, "I would like to present a new friend of ours from Sweden—Count Carl von Königsmark. Accounts of his heroic deeds reached my ears long since, and his Uncle Otto is so well known to most of us in this chamber that it is a double pleasure to welcome him to our Court."

As the Count bent over my hand, my eyes met the King's. He was smiling, and, when the touch of the young man's lips on my fingers brought that wretched flood of color into my face, he gave me an encouraging little nod.

"The Lady Ogle is new to Whitehall, too, my lord Count," he went on smoothly. "I hope you will both give me the pleasure of seeing you here again."

Then, leaving us together, he took his formal leave of the company and was gone. I had just begun an awkward little sentence about his Majesty's kindness when my grandmother bore down on us like a fighting ship in full sail. Giving me a cold frown and the Count a half nod, she took my arm and hurried me away.

Our parting was so abrupt, in fact, that I wondered afterwards if I had really heard him murmur, "We will meet again, my lady, very soon, I promise you!"

I wanted to question Lady Mary Sackville the moment I stepped into her coach the next morning, but I waited until we crossed Northumberland House's square cobbled courtyard and passed under the rampant stone Percy lion that guarded the archway into Charing Cross. Even then I let her tuck the fur robe more snugly around our feet, fuss over the hot bricks warming our toes, and jerk the leather window curtains back and forth until the morning sun did not shine directly into our eyes as we sat back on the padded squabs.

Finally, when the pretty, dark-eyed, dark-haired Countess of Dorset could find nothing else to do to make us more comfortable, I turned to her.

"Why are you taking me to Knole with you today, Lady Mary? So suddenly, I mean? I'm delighted to go, truly delighted, but I can't help wondering why."

My traveling companion looked at me with astonishment. "But—my dear child! Didn't your grandmother tell you?"

I shook my head. "I haven't seen her this morning. My chamberwoman waked me soon after dawn and said she had orders to have me dressed, packed, and ready to set out with you the moment you arrived. Grandam wasn't to be disturbed."

"Well!" Lady Mary looked even more astonished than before. "No wonder you are puzzled. How odd of Lady Percy! Why should she make such a mystery?"

"She probably never gave it a thought," I replied ruefully. "This is the way she always treats me—like a child. I'm ordered to do this or that, go here or there, but she rarely gives me a reason. I can usually figure things out for myself, but I'm completely baffled this time."

"No wonder. I would have been, too. Actually, my dear, there's a very good explanation. It seems that yesterday afternoon at Whitehall the King and the Duchess of Portsmouth were both quite insistent that you wed their little son, and when I saw Lady Percy later in the evening she was terribly concerned. Vehement, in fact; no Percy, she said, would marry a bastard—even the King's bastard. She told me that she had arranged your marriage with Lord Ogle to prevent just such a match, and she was not going to give in this time, either. That's why she wanted you out of town for a while, you see, and that's why I suggested taking you to Knole."

While she was talking, I remembered watching King Charles and Madame Louise with their small boy; I recalled that they had presented him to my grandmother, and I saw, again, the anger on her face. But I also remembered his Majesty's kindness to me and his gentle voice as he promised to be my friend.

"She's wrong to send me away," I told Lady Mary. "I'm sure she is. What she should do is allow me to see the King again and tell him myself how unhappy it would make me to wed his young son. I know he wouldn't force me against my will."

"Perhaps not," answered Lady Mary, "if the decision were his alone. But he's wax in the hands of his mistresses— they can have anything they ask for, as a rule. Portsmouth is always in debt, of course; and as she probably wants your fortune for herself and her boy, she'll nag at King Charles until he agrees. No"—she leaned over and patted my knee affectionately—"I think Lady Percy was right and I'm delighted to have you with me. I loved your mother very much —I still do, although I rarely see her—and I'm happy to have this opportunity to help her little daughter.

"As a matter of fact," she continued, smiling at me, "my only fear is that you may find it dull. We'll be quite alone, you see, because I'm going to Knole to put it in order; my husband has orders to remain away until all the work is finished. But I love the old house dearly, Lisa, and I'm hoping you will, too."

I assured her I would, and we both fell silent. For one thing it was rather difficult to talk in the jolting, swaying coach, and for another I suddenly realized that I was extremely weary. Yesterday's visit to Whitehall had been so full of excitement and nervous strain that I slept badly, and I think I had just dropped off into my first deep slumber when Dolly shook me awake with the news that we were to set out on this unexpected journey. I yawned in my corner, I saw Lady Mary yawning in hers, and before long we were both asleep.

We woke to find we had not made much progress; the roads were deeply rutted and pitted with holes, and we moved slowly and cautiously. A long nooning, welcomed by the tired horses and by us, well chilled and stiff by then, delayed us even more, so that it was almost dark by the time we reached Sevenoaks and drove up to the entrance of Knole.

In the shadowy dusk, and with lights gleaming at scores of windows, the rambling, irregular building looked to me like a fairy castle. Accustomed as I was to great houses, for Northumberland House, Petworth, Syon, and huge old Alnwick Castle were all part of my Percy inheritance, I was surprised and pleased to find this one so enchantingly different. Even at first glance, Knole had a charm all its own.

Our coach stopped with a jolt, as did the maids' vehicle behind us, and one of the footmen let down the steps and helped us to alight. A moment later we were inside the huge door facing a long double line of servants, drawn up to greet their mistress. While Lady Mary spoke to each by name I stood to one side, content to feel warmth creeping into my numb fingers and toes and hoping I could soon retire to my bedchamber and send for something hot to drink.

Although I was only half listening to my hostess, I realized that Lady Mary seemed mildly disturbed by something the steward said to her.

"The King's Bedroom for Lady Ogle?" As she questioned him she shook her dark curls in amused disapproval. "In this weather? Well, we'll see, Mr. Legge, we'll see. I thought perhaps one of the smaller chambers—but we won't upset your arrangements tonight, certainly."

She said nothing more until the housekeeper ushered us into a large crimson-walled room. When I gasped and blinked, Lady Mary laughed. It was not the elaborate tester bed with its glittering brocade hangings and great clumps of ostrich plumes at each corner that startled me; I had often slept in beds as richly decorated as this one. It was the other furniture that stunned and astonished me, for every piece was made of silver, heavy silver, intricately chased, molded, and polished until it gleamed and sparkled in the firelight.

"Vulgar, is it not?" Lady Mary was still chuckling, her soft brown eyes dancing as I stared around the room. "King James occupied this chamber many years ago, and the bed, with all its furnishings—see his cypher on the pillows?—was made just for his visit here. That's why we still call it the King's Bedroom. But my husband added these silver horrors. Ghastly, I think, although I've never said so to Charles. He's so proud of them! And just imagine the work, Lisa. It takes one woman all her time to keep them polished.

"Actually," she went on, "we use the room very seldom. But I did send a messenger ahead today saying that I was bringing the Countess of Ogle with me. Mr. Legge decided you should be here." Laughing again, she stepped nearer the hearth and held her hands to the leaping flames.

"Never mind, my dear. I promise to arrange matters more comfortably in the morning. The drafts here in winter are too much to be borne, but if you will be patient for this one night I will be very grateful. Once in bed—and we shall retire early—you should be quite warm." As she spoke the tapestry on one of the walls proved her point by stirring noticeably. "There's a cosy suite of small apartments nearer mine that we can ready for you tomorrow, so tell your woman to unpack as little as possible."

"I'm so happy to be here," I assured her, "that I shall be more than content anywhere. Tell Mr. Legge for me that I am greatly honored and will enjoy sleeping in King James's bed."

Lady Mary nodded and walked to the door. "When you have rested and changed we will have supper in my winter parlor. We need not stand on ceremony, thank God, as we are quite alone. No fuss, no banquets, no ladies and gentlemen squabbling—how delicious it is going to be!"

For the rest of February we did indeed have Knole to ourselves, and I found the peaceful interval fully as delicious as did Lady Mary. Putting this huge house in perfect order was, as she said, no mean task, and she certainly found much to be done. Chimneys needed sweeping and repairing, all the wainscoting was crying out for beeswax, many of the beautiful plaster ceilings were dark with smoke, and a multitude of smaller items wanted her attention.

I soon realized why my hostess had chosen this particular time for her annual visit; the empty house and dormant gardens freed most of the staff to help. It also gave her, she told me, the perfect opportunity to check the supply cupboards, stillroom, and linen closets, and she seemed pleased when I asked if I might not share in these pleasant chores.

"Lady Percy has never allowed me to take part in such matters," I said, "and I must confess that I'm woefully ignorant."

"I'm both surprised and shocked to hear it," Lady Mary answered. "Your grandmother knows that when you marry —or even if you don't marry again—the time will come when you must see to so many houses! And it is not enough, I assure you, to rely on your stewards and housekeepers." She shook her head gravely. "The lady of the manor, the chatelaine of the castle, the mistress of any home, however large or small, must know how things should be done or her people will slack and muddle. Why, during Charles's bachelor years the Dorset properties were so neglected that I almost wept when I began to restore them to order! I have often thought since that it was extremely wise of him to wed a widow instead of a green young maid."

"I think he was wise *and* lucky," I told her, wondering as I did so how Charles Sackville, the Earl of Dorset, had won this beautiful, capable, gentle woman. Even I had heard about his rackety past; a famous rake and libertine, he had been one of the leaders of London's wildest set of devil-may-care young noblemen, fighting, gambling, drinking, whoring, careering around the streets after dark, terrifying the watch, and ending up more often than not in the Round House.

Besides all this, he was a wit, poet, lover of the theater; a boon companion of Rochester, Sedley, and Buckingham, dissolute and notorious; and had the distinction of being Nell Gwyn's original protector—"My Charles the First," as she still calls him.

But I had also heard that middle age, succession to his earldom, and this happy marriage with Lady Mary had changed him. They said he was on the stout side, now, and inclined to think too much about his health. Gathering amusing people around his table had become his greatest pleasure, and he left the raking to younger men.

"We were both lucky," said Lady Mary. "My first marriage was a love match, and I am as happy in my second. If I could only bear Charles a child, I would have nothing more to wish for."

❧

On the morning after our arrival at Knole they moved me to a suite of charmingly decorated little rooms that opened off the Brown Gallery, and I was more comfortable there than I had ever been in all my life. The feathery trees and blue sky of the tapestries brought spring into my bed-chamber, the small curtained bed was soft and cosy, and the oak-paneled sitting room, overlooking the wintry gardens, soon seemed more my home than the large gloomy apartments at Northumberland House.

While Lady Mary was busy with her carpenters and

painters I wandered at will around the great building, trying to solve the puzzle of its unusual plan. Knole covered
four acres of ground, and all Lady Mary could tell me about
its involved geography was that it had seven courts, fifty-
two staircases, and three hundred and sixty-five rooms. "For
the days in the week, the weeks in the year, and the days in
a year. But you will often lose your way exploring them. I
still do."

As I look back, I realize that it was the evenings we spent
together that gave me the greatest pleasure. Never in the
fifteen years of my lonely life had I enjoyed the company
of a sympathetic, warmhearted friend and confidante, someone who was truly interested in the problems of my future
and the heartaches of my past, someone young enough to
understand my feelings and old enough to answer the
nagging questions that had embittered my dreams.

There were so many things I wanted to know about my
parents, things I had not dared ask my grandmother; now,
at last, I heard the answers.

"I was at Court when we learned that your father had
died in Italy," she told me, "and one of the first of your
mother's friends to see her after her return home. She was
heartbroken, bewildered—and no wonder. A ghastly experience! Losing her husband, then her unborn babe, then
having to bring Joscelyn's body all the way back to
England—"

As she related the story I began to remember something
of that awful journey. I was only four at the time, but I
found myself recalling dimly many days of jolting over hot,
dusty roads, then a weary voyage on a black-draped yacht.
And my mother weeping, holding me close in her arms.

"You were her only comfort," said Lady Mary. "She and
your father had set out for Italy without a care in the
world: rich, in love, their family increasing! She came home

—broken. And then to discover, as she soon did, that she would lose you too if she remarried!" Lady Mary sighed heavily and shook her head. "She hated your grandmother. I need not tell you why, I'm sure."

"But why did my father make such a will?" I asked. "Why couldn't my mother marry again and still be my guardian?"

"That will was made when he wed and was meant to ensure that his heir would spend his minority—if Joscelyn died young, as he did—on the Percy estates, and to safeguard the great Percy fortune from any fortune hunter who might court your mother. It wasn't that he didn't trust Betty, or expected to die.

"Betty vowed to me that she'd never give you up to Lady Percy," she continued. "She swore a dozen times that she'd remain single—that the thought of marrying again revolted her. But she was only twenty-four, so beautiful, and so very, very wealthy. Well, everything and everybody conspired against her and she finally lost you. From the moment she came back she was beseiged by suitors. Some wanted to marry her; others had less honorable intentions." She hesitated. "I must tell you that the King himself and his brother, the Duke of York, were among the latter."

I was shocked, horrified. What would I have done in such a situation?

"If she'd gone down to Petworth—?"

"She did. She retired to the country and refused to see anyone for months. But the most persistent of them followed her there, and her life became increasingly difficult. After three years she was so desperate that she took you to Paris and set up her residence there."

A warm flood of relief surged over me. My mother *had* wanted to keep me! Leaving all her friends, England—

"I remember Paris," I said thoughtfully. "Gray stone

buildings, narrow cobbled streets. Beautiful rooms and gardens and a dreadful smell from the Seine."

"And of course you know what happened there. But deeply as she loved Ralph Montagu, I don't think she would have married him if your grandmother had not promised that you could spend a large part of every year with them— a promise she broke immediately. Nor did Lady Percy keep her part of an agreement that any matrimonial plans for you must first be discussed with your mother."

This was some comfort, certainly, although I still felt that my mother should have prevented my marriage to Henry Ogle. "She should have gone to the King," I protested. "How *could* she let it happen?"

"She was in Paris and knew nothing of it until the knot was tied. Your stepfather was still ambassador there and demanded his wife's whole attention. No matter what he does, Betty has to think only of him and his children, and she's never been able to offer you a settled home here in England. As you can imagine, Lisa, this made it impossible for her to fight your grandmother for your custody."

"I see," I said slowly. "I really do see, Lady Mary. At last. I can never thank you enough for telling me all this. I've felt bitter—abandoned. I truly thought my mother didn't care what happened to me."

"She cared. Poor Betty. She's been an extremely unhappy woman, my dear child. In many ways."

It was surprising how swiftly the time fled. I woke one morning to the realization that Mary Sackville and I had been at Knole for almost three weeks, and I asked myself how much longer this pleasant interlude could last.

For one thing, all was now in order in the great house. The wainscots and furniture gleamed softly, the brass handles on the tall chests and the silver on the sideboards shone brightly, the chimneys no longer smoked, and the plaster ceilings were snowy white again. And, because I had helped with the task, I was well aware that the stillroom, linen closets, and supply cupboards were equally immaculate, their contents arranged tidily and listed in Lady Mary's housekeeping book. Even the brocade cushions, curtains, Turkish carpets, and tapestries had been freshened and mended.

I was breakfasting with Lady Mary when she answered the question for me.

"I wrote Charles yesterday," she said, "telling him that all was done here at last and that we would return to town very soon. We might even set out tomorrow if the weather stays clear." Rising, she strolled to the window and looked up. "But I don't like that sky. It may mean snow." She returned to the table and smiled at me. "I sent the same message to Lady Percy, Lisa, but I shall hate giving you up to her. I'd like to keep you with me forever and defy the King and the fortune hunters—or keep you, at least, until we can find you a handsome, delightful husband."

"I wish you could," I replied wistfully. "I've never been so happy, Lady Mary. Never."

3

We were studying the sky again later that day, and discussing the possibility of leaving Knole in the morning, when a sudden noise in the entrance hall made us hush and listen.

"Now who could that be?" asked Lady Mary, sounding very exasperated. "I hope it isn't anyone who will disturb our last quiet evening together!"

As she spoke a lackey ran into the Brown Gallery where we had been sitting.

"The master, milady!" he announced excitedly. "His lordship has just arrived with two other gentlemen."

We hurried into the Great Hall and found three men grouped near the fire with wine goblets in their hands. The Earl of Dorset set his down and strode to meet his wife; while he was embracing her, I glanced at his two guests. One, a man of about fifty, was a stranger. The other, to my astonishment, was Count Königsmark, the Swedish gallant I had met at Whitehall. I suppose my surprise was obvious, for he looked very amused as our eyes met, and he gave me a tiny nod that seemed to say, I told you I would see you soon!

"This is an unexpected pleasure, Charles," said Lady Mary when her husband released her.

"An impulse, my dear, an impulse! When your message arrived yesterday I decided to ride down and escort you back to London. And, as the Court has moved to Windsor, leaving the city a dull place, I was able to persuade our good friend John Dryden here—" he waved his pudgy hand at the older of the two men—"and my new acquaintance, Count Königsmark from Sweden, to bear me company.

"Actually, it might not have occurred to me if our neighbors the Selbys had not been journeying to Ightham today," he went on, "George's lady was fretting about some wild tale of highwaymen on the roads, so I suggested that we ride beside her coach."

"In that case," said Lady Mary, sweeping a curtsy to her guests, "Lady Ogle and I are much obliged to Mistress Selby for her timidity. Highwaymen or no, my lord, we will be exceedingly happy to have your escort back to town." Turning, she drew me forward. "Charles you know, of course, and Mr. Dryden is an old friend of—"

"An old friend," interrupted Mr. Dryden, raising quizzical eyebrows and smiling at me, "*and* by way of being kin to Lady Ogle. We are cousins, my lady."

"Cousins, sir?" I had often heard of the famous playwright, but never that we were related. All I had been told was that his plays were too coarse for my eyes and ears.

"Cousins by marriage," he replied. "Your grandmother is the dowager Countess of Northumberland, born a Howard. My wife was named Lady Elizabeth Howard, too, Lady Percy's cousin."

I saw a look of relief flash across Lady Mary's face. She told me later she knew nothing of the relationship and had had a moment's concern about presenting Mr. Dryden to me. Now, as she turned to Count Königsmark, he stepped forward and claimed my acquaintance, making a handsome leg and raising my hand to his lips.

"We did not come to disturb your household," said Lord Dorset. "I warned Dryden and Königsmark that we would find a skeleton staff and a house under Holland covers. All we want, my love, is supper, a night's sleep, and breakfast. We will be happy to set out again the moment you are ready."

"Our plan was to leave here by midmorning," answered Lady Mary, a little hesitantly, "and you are quite right about the house. Most of it is already closed. We could, of course, change all that—"

"No, no. Leave everything as it is. A start by midmorning will suit us perfectly, won't it, gentlemen? With luck we can dine at Chiselhurst—the inn there sets a good table—and reach London in good season."

❧

But we did not leave Knole the next day. We awakened to find that it had been snowing most of the night, and the storm was growing worse. After a hasty glance out of the window through thickly falling flakes at a white, white world, I, for one, climbed immediately back into the shelter of my comfortable little bed and pulled the coverlet up around my shoulders, determined to stay there for the present.

Dolly, bringing in my breakfast a few minutes later, told me that we could not think of setting out that morning. "The roads are quite impassable," she said rather gleefully, "and the steward, who is a great hand at predicting the weather, thinks it will keep on snowing for at least another twenty-four hours."

As she talked, she set my tray on a small table and handed me my chamber robe. "You never saw such a bustle as is going on below stairs!" she went on. "Her ladyship has been down for hours already, making sure we have enough wood and food in the house. Poor lady! It was quite enough, having my lord arrive all unexpected with a party, just after the maids had stripped the beds and stuffed the chimneys. Now cook is in a dreadful taking, and who can blame her? Three kitchen maids sent home yesterday to visit their families—the staff here always have a decent holiday when the house is closed—and she says the master will be wanting fancy sauces and scores of jellies and pastries."

While I ate, Dolly moved around the pretty bedchamber, setting it in order for the day. It was obvious that she, at least, was enjoying the unusual situation. "Four of the strongest men are on their way to the home farm," she continued, "with orders to bring back everything they can carry. Milk, eggs, capons, ducks, a suckling pig—oh, we won't starve, I promise you, despite the grumbling in the kitchen."

"I don't see why we should," I remarked. "There are only five of us and part of the staff. The storm can't last forever." In my heart I wished it would; I was dreading my return to Northumberland House and Lady Percy. It was a delightful adventure, being shut up here at Knole with the easygoing Sackvilles, a famous playwright, and a handsome, charming young man; the longer that adventure lasted the happier I would be.

Eager to see for myself what was going on elsewhere, I finished my cold beef and crusty bread and hurried into my clothes, pretending that I had chosen my blue velvet gown only because it was warm. It was, of course, my most becoming garment, and a final glance in the mirror sent me off not too dissatisfied with my appearance. The peaceful weeks had added color to my cheeks and a little roundness to my thin face, and even my hated red hair seemed less objectionable. How fortunate that my grandmother had not thought it necessary for me to wear that hideous mourning robe at Knole!

I remember I was actually singing as I ran down the wide, heavily carved and painted staircase and sought out Lady Mary. I found her in a hive of activity, but her voice, issuing one order after another, was as soft as usual and her smiles as frequent. The grumbling that Dolly had mentioned must have been swept away by her kindness and good humor, for there was no sign of it now; instead there was much laughing and chaffing among the servants, hastening here and there at her bidding.

"Won't you put me to work, too?" I asked, after watching the busy scene for a few minutes.

"Gladly," was Lady Mary's prompt reply. "Go and oversee the men who are opening the Leicester Gallery for us. It occurred to me that its crimson velvet and damask would at least *look* warm."

When I reached the long narrow room I found one of the lackeys stripping off the linen covers while another moved from one wall sconce to another, setting fresh wax candles in place. They had already unstuffed the huge fireplace chimney, and a good hot fire was blazing on the hearth; everything seemed in such order that I was at a loss to find anything more to be done.

My only suggestion was that our small company might be more comfortable if some of the chairs and crimson-covered couches were drawn into a circle around the fire, and I was standing back and admiring the result when Count Carl entered the gallery.

"So here you are, my lady." He beamed down on me, his blue eyes lighting up as they met mine. "They say we remain at Knole, which is very, very good news for me!"

His speech was still awkward enough to mark him a foreigner, but he rarely had to hesitate long for the right word or phrase. I learned later that he had made other earlier visits to England and had studied our language as a boy.

"Master Dryden tells me it is unusual to have such a heavy snow at this time of year and that the March winds will pile it high over the roads. When this happens in Sweden we shrug our shoulders, find our warmest cloaks, order what you call sledges out of the stables, and go about our business. But here we remain in the house. What shall we do? My lord is listening to his friend's newest play and sent me to amuse the ladies. Command me!"

I looked at the clock. Dinner would not be served for two hours, and I was at a loss for an answer until I saw a backgammon board set up. Count Carl admitted that he had played once or twice and I, having been ordered to the table whenever my grandmother needed an opponent, suggested we try a game, resigning myself to the prospect of a dull contest with an unskilled beginner. To my surprise he proved a good pupil and a good gamester, mastering the fine points of strategy in no time, and when the others came in we were just finishing a hard-fought battle.

The rest of the day passed swiftly and pleasantly. Cards, music, amusing talk—I could never remember having laughed so much or enjoyed myself so completely. Any remnant of my shyness disappeared early, and by bedtime I felt as if I had always known these delightful people.

After a sound night's sleep I awakened to find that although the snow had stopped the temperature had dropped sharply; there was ice on the well, the ropes were frozen tight to the windlass, and the snow covering everything was glazed over with an icy crust. Great pails of it were being melted in the kitchen to provide us with water, and one of the lackeys, Dolly told me, had gone "arse over kettle" on his way back to the house.

To my great relief this new shift in the weather made our return to town even more impossible, and I enjoyed the others with a light heart. For no apparent reason, however, the relaxed mood of the day before had disappeared, and the men were so restless by midmorning that we were ready to cheer when a servant ushered in George Selby, the neighbor with whom Charles and his guests had traveled from London.

"By God!" said my host, jumping to his feet. "We are glad to see you, George! My lady was just calling us caged beasts, and with good reason. But how did you get here, man? We were told the roads are drifted solid and the fields a glare of ice."

Selby, a stout little man with a round, red face, laughed at him. "In a sledge, of course. You've spent too many winters in town, Charles."

"A sledge! I never thought of that," exclaimed Lady Mary, after she presented him to me. "We've been trapped here, thinking we could not venture out. Have we a sledge, my lord?"

"We must have," answered her husband a little sheepishly. "We did, certainly, some years ago. I'll inquire immediately."

"If it's not in order you must ride back to the Mote with me," said the newcomer, settling into a chair by the fire and stretching his short legs out onto the hearth. "I have strict orders from my wife to bring you all back to dinner, and I don't dare show my face without you. We want company, so don't say no."

"You don't need to urge us, sir. We'll come with pleasure!"

"Splendid, splendid! But you must wrap up well and wear your thickest boots; the sledge has a canvas top, straw for our feet, and bricks that we'll have your people reheat, my lady. Oh, and bring your skates. I left two men sweeping the snow off the lake."

Lady Mary shivered. "You won't lure me out on the ice, George. But I did see several pairs when I was turning out a cupboard near the stillroom."

"I don't suppose I've forgotten how," said Charles. "What about you, John? And you, Lisa? I don't ask you, Carl. I know that all Swedes skate almost before they walk."

"I've never tried," replied Master Dryden. "I'm afraid I'm too old now."

"Of course you're not," said Carl firmly. "I'll teach you in no time. And you, Lady Ogle?"

"I've been on the ice at Petworth once or twice, but I'm not very skillful. Perhaps I should stay with Lady Mary by the fire."

He shook his blond head vigorously. "No, no. You will be a bird, wait and see."

A conference with the head stableman revealed that the Knole sledge did indeed need a few hours' work to put it into repair, so we climbed into Master Selby's waiting vehicle and set out for Ightham Mote. The wooden runners skimmed swiftly over the snow, and almost before the bricks at our feet had time to lose their heat we reached our destination.

As I scrambled out of the queer arklike thing, I saw that we were in a courtyard bounded by an unusually wide moat; facing us was a handsome manor house with an entrance opening into a tall tower. A hail from our host, who had hurried ahead, took us over the threshold, where we found ourselves in a huge banqueting hall, being welcomed by Mistress Selby.

She sat us down at the table almost immediately, and after a bit of the customary polite conversation her husband turned to Carl and asked him to tell us about his adventures with the Moors. "I've heard it's quite a story," Master Selby said.

Indeed it was. Carl began his tale at once, and I, for one, was soon almost holding my breath. As a lad of nineteen, he had ventured out with the Knights of St. John in their galley. "We were chasing a pirate craft," he said, "and when we caught up with it I boarded it alone, thinking the others were right behind me. I clung to a cable with one hand and slashed at the dark-skinned Moors with the other. Then, to my horror, I saw that our galley had been driven off and there I was, a lone Christian, fighting a shipload of infidels!"

I think I gasped aloud. I know I felt the color come and go in my cheeks, he made the account of his danger so vivid, so frightening.

"They cut through the cable I was holding with a yataghan," he went on, his blue eyes flashing with excitement, "and I plunged into the sea, weighed down by my heavy cutlass and helmet. They thought me drowned, of course, but I struggled through the waves to my comrades' craft, clambered aboard, and shouted to them to renew the attack. The sight of me standing on the prow of our galley, unharmed, threw the Moors into a panic and they actually blew up their ship!"

When we exclaimed and applauded, Carl threw back his head and laughed, looking so handsome that my heart skipped a beat. The Moors must have thought him a god, I decided; he was exactly as I would imagine Mars to be.

When we left the gentlemen with their wine, Mistress Selby took Lady Mary and me to freshen up, then sent me off to look at the chapel that dated back to Henry VIII. when I returned, I heard them talking about Carl and I stopped, shocked and horrified.

"What a braggart!" Mistress Selby was saying. "Did you see his face? He was gloating over his prowess, Lady Mary—gloating!"

"Don't forget that he's a foreigner," replied Lady Mary. "An Englishman wouldn't boast in that manner, I grant you. But Count Carl is not an Englishman, after all, and he's been a most charming guest."

Lady Mary's words took some of the sting out of Mistress Selby's comments, and I joined them quickly before anything more was said, not wanting to eavesdrop. I was still disturbed when it was time to tie on my skates, but the crisp air, the gay talk, and the friendly attitude of the other men toward Carl made me tell myself that Mistress Selby was a stupid old woman and that I was silly to pay any attention to her thoughtless criticism.

I was struggling to my feet, looking down at the clumsy strips of metal that curled up over my toes like a jester's shoes, as he skated to my side. With a sigh of relief, I put my hands in his and let him pull me erect. For a moment we stood there, glancing around us; the sun was shining now, turning the whole scene into a glinting, gleaming fairyland. The frozen lake, the snow-laden branches of the trees edging it, the sparkling crust on the nearby bowling green all enchanted my eyes.

"Is this the way Sweden looks in winter?" I asked him.

"Not quite," he replied. "Sweden is bolder, grander. Almost solemn in its white, white stillness. This"—he swept a gauntleted hand around the little pond and its surroundings—"this is a toy world, compared to mine. So dainty, so pretty, so charming!" His eyes plunged into mine, seeming to say that he found me dainty, pretty, and charming too, and as we moved onto the ice I felt shy and awkward.

"Careful," Carl warned me, "Slowly, slowly." We struck out together, he gliding easily, I wobbling in a frightening manner.

"Help!" My feet shot out from under me. I clutched him frantically and gave a scream of laughter. "Don't let me fall —don't let me fall!"

But instead of landing on the ice, as I expected, I found myself righted immediately. A strong arm swept me back into position, my feet came together, my head went up, and he clasped my hands even more firmly in his.

"Slowly!" he repeated. "Slowly! One foot ahead, now the other—better, better. Again. One foot ahead, now the other—slowly, slowly."

Before I believed it possible my feet were moving smoothly with his. We circled the small lake in a careful, leisurely way; once, twice, then a third time, but more swiftly as I gained balance and confidence. Now that I was not feverishly preoccupied with my feet, I glanced over at our friends, who seemed to be doing more laughing than skating.

Dryden, with the Earl of Dorset on one side and Master Selby on the other, a desperate arm around their necks and both of his feet in the air, was pleading loudly to be helped back to shore.

"Stop your laughing, you zanies," he bellowed. "Help me off this damn stuff before I break my neck!"

"Before you break ours, you mean. Come on, John—try, man, try!"

"I promised to teach him, did I not?" said Carl, smiling down at me. "Suppose I give you to Charles for a turn, and I'll see what I can do?"

Skating with the Earl was pleasant but rather dull. It was true that we moved around the ice without disaster, but there was an awkwardness and lack of rhythm. While we tried to match our strides, my new partner told me of his youth at Knole and his long friendship with George Selby. I countered with a description of my lonely years at Petworth. "My visit to Knole," I told him gratefully, "has been the happiest time of my life. I shall hate to have it end."

"And so will Mary," he replied. "She was saying so last night. By God, I wouldn't have believed it!" Giving a whistle of surprise, he nodded his head at the others. "Look, my lady. Königsmark has Dryden actually skating!"

Sure enough, the playwright was on his feet, wavering a little but erect, and although the other two men were beside him they were not supporting him as they had done before. He gave a triumphant shout when he saw us watching him.

"Look! How's this?" and off he went, knees bent, skates flashing in the sun. A moment later, while we held our breath, I saw one leg falter; he went down with a crash, flailing madly as he fell.

Shaking with laughter we gathered around him, lifting him up.

"Beautiful! It was swanlike," said Charles. "Try again, Dryden."

But our friend had had enough and he said so. He managed to reach the bank, sat down, and began to untie his skates.

"Perhaps he's right," announced Charles, nodding. "My legs tell me that I'm older than I think. Wait for me, John, and I'll go back to the house with you. Some of Mistress

Selby's mulled wine and a chair close to the fire will more than content me for a while."

"If I may have one more turn with Lady Ogle," said Carl, "we will join you."

"Hurry, then," Charles ordered. "The sun is dropping, we've had the best of the day, and my lady would have our heads if we left you two alone here."

So while the three older men stamped around on the bank, Carl led me back on the ice. At his suggestion we crossed our hands this time, and away we went, bending and swooping in perfect harmony, round and round and round. It was delicious, it was exhilarating, it was sheer heaven! Could anything be more exciting than this? I wanted to shout, to sing—

At that very moment Carl burst into a Swedish skating song and swung me along in time to it, almost as if we were dancing. I looked up into his face and gave a laugh that was really a crow of joy. His eyes laughed back at mine, his hands tightened, and I felt a oneness with him, a wonderful closeness that made words unnecessary; it was as if he knew what I was thinking and was telling me so with his hands and eyes.

Then, just before we glided back to where our friends were waiting, Carl stopped singing and slowed our skates. He bent a little and spoke softly into my ear. "Only here on the ice have I had you to myself," he murmured caressingly. "And for such a short minute. We must arrange something. . . ."

An hour or so later, when our Knole party had climbed into our waiting sledge, repaired now and ready to take us home, I remembered the odd, husky way Carl had spoken of having me to himself. Just thinking about it sent a warm tingle through my body. I tried to see his face in the dimness. He was sitting beside me, but he was talking to Lady Mary and seemed unaware of our closeness.

Or so I assumed until the shadows under the canvas hood turned to inky blackness. Suddenly I felt something slip under the fur rug wrapped around me. My thick leather glove was pulled off and a warm hand enveloped mine, holding it tight. I knew I should take mine away—indeed, I did give one little halfhearted tug—but when the long, strong fingers merely closed even more firmly I must confess I left them there.

That warm tingle was now an all-encompassing glow, and I seemed to be drifting on a soft, rapturous cloud that almost blotted out the voices around me. I knew we would reach Knole too soon—all too soon! With a tiny, quickly smothered sigh of happiness, I curled my fingers around Carl's and nestled closer to his tall shoulder in that blessed, merciful dark.

4

Our afternoon on the ice left us in a satisfied, almost languid mood. All signs of restlessness were gone, and the men seemed more than willing to sup quietly, yawn, and chat for an hour or two around the fire in the Leicester Gallery.

Probably because my senses were still stirred by the intimacy of the ride back from Ightham Mote, I took very little part in the easy talk. Sunk deep in a cushioned chair, I relived those moments in the sledge; even recollecting them sent that same delicious tingle up and down my spine, and every time my eyes met Carl's, which was often, I was sure his thoughts were not so different from mine.

When, finally, John Dryden rose to his feet and announced that he was for bed, there was no protest from the rest of the company.

"I, for one," said Charles, "am more than ready. All that brisk air was too much for me. Coming, my love?"

Lady Mary's nod and smile were the signal for me to rise, too, and in a flash Carl was at my side with my candlestick in his hand. While the others, moving more slowly, were taking theirs from the table by the door, he bent over me and whispered, "Come back here after everyone is in bed."

Realizing that the treacherous color was dyeing my cheeks, I walked a little ahead of the rest, shading my candle flame with one hand. By the time I reached the door to my rooms I was sufficiently composed to wish my friends good night in my usual voice.

Once inside my bedchamber I fought a losing battle with my conscience, knowing perfectly well that I should *not* do as Carl had suggested. That I intended to return to the Gallery, however, was undeniable, and all that remained was to decide how long to wait and what excuse to give for leaving my rooms again.

The simplest was probably the best; a book. But as the natural thing would be to send Dolly for it, I would have to tell her I wanted to choose one for myself.

This being settled, I dawdled back into my pretty sitting room and picked up my needlework. "I'm not a bit sleepy," I said to Dolly, "I'll work on my tapestry for a while."

When thirty slow minutes had passed I threw it down and rose. "I'm still wide awake," I told her. "I'll find a book and read in bed."

"I don't like it, my lady." Dolly clucked her disapproval, and frowned at me. "One of these nights you'll set the bedcurtains afire." As she always said this, I made no answer; instead, I drifted around the chamber, picking up one book after another.

"These are all so dull!" I murmured. "I'll slip back to the gallery and find something else." And, before Dolly could protest, I had my candlestick in my hand and was on my way.

All was dark and quiet as I hurried through the deserted

rooms. The servants, I knew, had been ordered to go to bed themselves soon after their master and mistress retired. This was another of Lady Mary's considerate rules; at Petworth, Northumberland House, and Syon, a good third of our staff must, by my grandmother's command remain on duty for two hours after the rest of the house was abed.

Even so, I breathed more easily when I reached the Leicester Gallery and closed the door behind me. The long room was empty, the dying fire flickering very faintly on the wainscoting and crimson cushions; the rows of portraits were lost in the shadows.

As a precaution, I took the first book I saw and tucked it under my arm. Then, as I often did in this particular chamber, I walked down the gallery and stood for moment looking at the portrait of James I. It was, I thought, the most fascinating of all the pictures at Knole, and more honest in its likeness of that homely, stumbling, stuttering king than any I had seen elsewhere. But actually what brought me back to it, time after time, was the fact that the red velvet chair in which he had been painted was sitting right under the picture itself, the velvet a bit worn by the years but still intact.

A footstep sounded behind me, a hand took my candle away, and another removed my book. An instant later the same hands swung me around and I was in Carl's arms, being ruthlessly and thoroughly kissed. First he kissed my mouth, long deep kisses that set me aflame; then, when I gasped and tried to pull away, he laughed softly and set his lips to wandering from my mouth to my cheeks, my closed eyelids, the nape of my neck—and back to my lips again.

Suddenly I pressed closer and closer to him, and now it was Carl who drew away, caressing my hair with a gentle hand.

"*Mitt hjärta, mitt hjärta!*" At first he whispered the sweet-sounding words to me in Swedish, then in my own tongue. "My heart, my heart! Here in my arms at last." And again his lips strayed around my throat until I quivered and clung to him.

Finally, with a trembling sigh, he raised his head and led me to a seat by the fading fire.

"I could love you forever," he told me, "but there is something to say and who knows whether we will have another meeting alone? Let me talk quickly, kiss you good night, and send you away."

I waited, too shaken to speak.

"As you see, *mitt hjärta*, I have—how is it?—fallen in love. I asked myself that day at Westminster, is not this the one for me, so beautiful in your black against the red chest? And here, so delicious in every way! At the backgammon board, clever; as a fledgling swan, adorable. Now, having held you in my arms, I know for sure. You will be my wife, yes?"

By the time he finished I was in a state of bewildered rapture. Could this possibly be happening to me? To *me*? This man—handsome, brave, kind—wanting to marry me? I had dreamed it. My head whirled.

"But—I cannot say yes," I replied at last, sounding shy. "Or no. Lady Percy is my guardian. She arranges my life—always!"

"This I know," Carl said calmly. "Do not let this disturb your heart. I shall go to the great Lady Percy—dragons do not frighten me, you know. I will say, 'Here I am, a suitor for the hand of your lovely granddaughter.' And she will ask me who I am. So, I shall tell her. What could be more simple? It arranges itself!"

I looked at him in wonderment. Well, perhaps he was right. The confidence in his voice, his possessive arms, the way he kissed me good night and sent me off to bed all made me think he could win over my grandmother.

I awoke the next morning with my confidence unshaken. My only question was whether or not to tell my secret to Lady Mary. There never seemed to be a good opportunity, however, and when the cold snap ended and the snow began to thaw I had still not spoken.

The great problem now, of course, was when we could all return to London; we were actually discussing it when a lackey entered the dining hall and announced that a Lady Lucy Hay had arrived and wished to see Lady Mary.

"Lady Lucy Hay! Here? Bring her to us immediately."

Stunned by the news, I raised frightened eyes to my love, who happened to be beside me at the table. His answering smile was reassuring, but the sight of Lady Lucy, limping in a few minutes later, weary, distraught, and travel-stained, brought back my fears.

Her first words made matters worse. "I've come to carry Lisa off to Petworth. Urgent business there made it necessary for Lady Percy to set out at dawn this morning—the first day the roads have been clear enough—and I started for here in a second coach at the same time."

"But you must be exhausted!" said Lady Mary, filling a goblet with wine.

"We stuck in the mud three times," my cousin admitted in her timid, quavering voice. "The trip from here to Petworth will be dreadful, but Lady Percy will be angry if we waste a moment on the way. She ordered me to continue the journey as soon as the horses were rested."

Everyone argued with her, insisting that she needed a night's sleep before setting out again, but her fear of my grandmother was too strong. The minute we rose from the table she took me off to my rooms and watched me change into traveling garments while Dolly packed my boxes. Lady

Mary, openly distressed at this sudden end to my happy visit, bustled in and out with little comforts to ease our long ride.

Needless to say, I did not have a second alone with Carl, and I settled into my corner of the mud-spattered coach with nothing to cling to but the memory of his kiss on my fingers, as he said farewell, and the sound of his voice saying firmly, as he had at Whitehall, "We will meet again very soon!"

&

The days and nights that intervened before we pulled into the cobbled courtyard at Petworth were a nightmare. I can still feel the cold that crept into our bones as we jolted over the rough roads, taste the poor food in the country inns, shiver at the memory of the damp beds, the lumpy mattresses. Reluctant as I was to resume life under my grandmother's domination, I could not wish this particular journey prolonged.

I alighted from the coach with a heavy heart, dreading our meeting. To my great relief, she had already retired for the night, having only just arrived at Petworth herself, and I ran up to my room eager to see my dear Whiskers again after the long months since I had last held her in my arms.

She was on her cushion near the hearth, but I did not receive the warm welcome for which I hoped: one amber eye opened when I touched the furry, sleeping mound of white and orange; then, after a cold stare, it closed and she tucked her head back into the circle of paws and tail.

It was not until I was in bed and the chamber darkened for the night that my little pet decided to forgive me for deserting her. Dolly had, in fact, just closed the door behind her when there was a thump on the satin coverlet and four feet padded up the bed. Smiling in the dimness, I bent my head and was given a small kiss by a tiny rough tongue. That done, Whiskers flopped down, curled up in the curve of my body, and began to purr. Content for the moment, I shut out my anxieties and drifted off to sleep.

With my breakfast the next morning came a message that Lady Percy would be busy until time for our noonday dinner. Determined to make the most of this short reprieve, I dressed warmly, hurried out of the house, and crossed the wide stretch of lawn to the willow-edged lake. The deer, grazing on the brownish grass so recently covered with snow, lifted their heads to look at me with soft eyes, then resumed their nibbling. Hunting was not allowed at Petworth, and our deer had no reason to fear us.

Thinking wistfully of my happy skating lesson at Ightham Mote, I walked to the bank of the large sheet of ornamental water. It shimmered and rippled at me in the early spring sunshine, with only a hint of ice here and there among the willow roots. It was difficult to recapture the delight of that exhilarating afternoon, so I turned and made my way back to the house, its tower and rows of dormered windows looking bleak as I approached.

Instead of circling it and entering the front door that led into the Great Hall, I slipped through the small entrance to the chapel. Finding it empty, I knelt and tried to pray. In my present state of mind I found it impossible to be very coherent, sending heavenward an almost wordless plea for help. How God could help Carl and me I did not know, I could only ask.

I was wiping away a few desolate tears when I heard my grandmother's sharp voice in the adjacent winter parlor, berating the steward for some carelessness she had just uncovered. Not wanting her to see my reddened eyes, I crept into the small chamber known to us as the King's Room and climbed up the narrow wooden staircase to the

Queen's Room directly overhead. These were odd old chambers, rarely occupied in these days, and because the fires were never lighted in them they were colder and damper than the outdoors.

Despite my heavy cloak I shivered. Hoping that my grandmother would not remain below too long, I drifted to one of the windows and glanced idly around the wintry landscape, down on the garden with its stiff pattern of flower beds and still fountain, over the bowling green to the rose garden, and beyond into the walled kitchen garden. Then I shifted my gaze and looked past the row of village houses on the other side of our high wall and on up North Street which they bordered.

Suddenly I stiffened, my eyes unbelieving. A lone rider was trotting slowly down the street, a broad-shouldered, slender man, hatless, with a mass of long pale-gold hair gleaming in the thin sunshine.

Although he was just entering the village, I was almost sure it was Carl. Who else in the world had a shoulder-length cloak of fair hair? Without waiting to be certain, I ran, my heart pounding, down the stairs and into the garden, past the separate buildings that housed the kitchens and the coal and wood supplies, through the gate in the wall, and out into North Street, to the village church, only a stone's throw away. I slipped into the sheltered doorway and waited breathlessly. The horseman was approaching, his mount held to a walk. He was looking from right to left as if uncertain of his whereabouts or destination, and when he reached the Little White Hart Inn he pulled up, dismounted, tied his horse to the hitching post, and disappeared inside.

Keeping carefully out of sight, I saw him come out with Henry Rice, the inn victualer. Rice pointed down the road past the church, indicating the gatehouse of Petworth

Manor, and then, to my great relief, bowed, smiled, re-entered the inn, and closed the door behind him. As far as I could see there was now no one in sight but the golden-haired man on the large black stallion.

And it *was* Carl! I ran instantly out to the side of the road and hailed him, my hood falling back on my shoulders as I waved a gloved hand.

"My lady! Lisa!" In a flash he was off his horse again, his bright blue eyes gleaming with surprised delight.

"Take your mount around the rear," I told him quickly, "and join me inside the church. It's always deserted at this time of day."

He was obeying me before I finished speaking; I pushed open the church door and went inside, praying that it would be empty. Finding that it was, I turned back to wait in the little vestibule.

The door creaked open and I was in Carl's arms.

I pushed him away at last and tried, with trembling fingers, to smooth my red curls into some order. "We must talk, Carl," I said. "Perhaps we'd be safer in the priest's hole."

"Priest's hole?"

I nodded, leading the way. "There's a way into it from our private gallery," I told him. "It was a chamber for a 'Mass priest' at one time—a room where pilgrims and travelers could hear very early Mass when they were passing through Petworth. Later it became unlawful to shelter priests, and someone concealed the entrance in that paneling."

We had reached the little gallery. Running my fingers over the carving on the wall, I pressed a leaf. A panel slid open, we stepped inside a tiny stone-walled chamber, and I closed the panel again.

"Tell me everything," I demanded.

He laughed down into my eyes. "Everything? Well, first I am shocked when you are torn from me at Knole. So I count on my fingers the days before you reach Petworth. I ride back to London, I see my young brother Philip at his school there, I have a short audience with the King. Then I climb on my horse and turn his nose this way. After another kiss or two I shall go boldly through the gate which the innkeeper showed me and ask to see Lady Percy."

"But, Carl—" Despite his confident face and smiling eyes I could not feel that everything was as simple as he thought it. "I hope my grandmother will listen to you, but suppose she says no?"

"No? Why should she? I am a Königsmark!"

"She refused King Charles when he wanted me to marry one of his sons, and she's sneered at offers from many other noblemen."

He shrugged his wide shoulders. "If she should be so stupid I must make her change her mind. So, *mitt hjärta*, will you take me to this Percy lioness, who does not frighten me at all, or shall I go to her alone as I had planned?"

For a moment I considered this in silence. "I think," I said slowly, "that it would be wiser for me to know nothing of your arrival. If she knew that I had run out and hailed you, down here in the village street—!"

"Then we are foolish to linger and risk discovery. I shall be off, leaving you to pray for my success and our happiness."

Somehow I made myself remain away from the house for the better part of an hour. Then, taking my courage in my shaking hands, I sought out my grandmother in the comfortable withdrawing room over the Great Hall. She was alone, her face grim.

"So!"

Her greeting was in the sneering, pouncing voice that al-

ways made me feel ill, and her eyes reminded me of a cat
viewing a mouse and gloating at the prospect of a little
torture.

"So you found yourself a suitor at Knole?" Pausing, she
raked me from head to foot with her prominent eyes. "And
a most arrogant, argumentative, cocksure young man! He
speaks English well for a Swede, but he finds it difficult to
understand our small word *no*."

I swallowed. "A Swede?"

"Oh, come, Lisa! Don't waste my time. You know perfectly well that I mean Count Carl Königsmark, who apparently sneaked down to Knole, having heard of your
fortune. He walked in here an hour ago and demanded your
hand in marriage, insisting that a Königsmark is a suitable
match for a Percy. Well, he knows better now. He won't
dare try to see you again, I promise you, nor bother me with
his wild protestations."

I could not speak.

"And if you have a soft spot for that handsome rascal,
Elizabeth, forget it. I'm sending you to Paris with Lucy the
moment it can be arranged, where you'll stay until I've
chosen another husband for you. The King has been pressing
me again on behalf of his little bastard—and this morning's
interview with that other fortune hunter makes it even more
imperative that you leave England immediately."

 5

As I proceeded up the stairs and through the rabbit's warren of small, dark rooms that led to the royal salon, I found myself holding my breath. Lady Lucy, just behind me, voiced her disgust.

"I thought Whitehall putrid," she said, "but this French palace makes it seem like a rose garden!"

"I don't see how King Louis can stand it." I paused for a moment by an open window and looked down on the Seine, hoping for a breath of fresher air. "No wonder Queen Marie-Thérèse is at St. Germain! Faugh! It's even fouler here than it was below, and I thought all Paris had been using *that* floor for a garderobe. There's a different and more revolting odor up here."

The wife of the English Ambassador to France, our guide today, came to the window and sniffed. "That particular stench," she told me, "is from the butchers' markets nearby. The wind must be in the worst possible direction." Reaching into her reticule, she pulled out a scented handkerchief and held it over her nose. "As for the King, you may be sure, Lady Ogle, that he is only too eager to see the last of this dreadful old Louvre. Versailles will be finished soon, thank God, and then Louis will live as a king should. They say there won't be a palace in the world to compare with it."

A large gilt clock on the opposite wall struck nine. She sighed.

"Oh, dear! I'm afraid we must hurry on. King Louis's guests are supposed to gather in the salon before the end of the next quarter hour. Not that his Majesty will have honored us by then. He often lingers in Madame de Maintenon's rooms until ten."

"Madame de Maintenon? I thought the royal favorite was Marie de Fontage." We were moving up the stairs again, following a large stream of richly garbed ladies and gentlemen. "Of course, my three weeks in Paris have been so quiet I know nothing of the Court gossip."

"The little Fontage was discarded months ago, my dear. As a matter of fact, she is extremely ill and may well be dying. But as for Maintenon"—the Ambassadress shrugged her plump shoulders—"the story is that she is *not* Louis's mistress. They say she has brought about a kind of reconciliation between the King and Queen and that it is her good influence that makes the Court such a different place."

"In what way?"

"Oh, everyone must be very moral now. The days of royal debauchery and lavish balls are past, as you will soon see. His Majesty entertains his guests with these quiet suppers."

I laughed ruefully. "Apparently I am never to see or share in the gay madness I thought an inseparable part of a royal court. There's nothing but card playing at home now, you know. Whitehall, St. James's—it's all a game called basset."

By this time we had reached the antechamber of the King's supper room; here an usher took us in charge and led us directly into the inner chamber and to one of the long tables. The air was still heavy but it seemed a little sweeter, a mixture of the good food smells rising from steaming platters already set out on sideboards and the strong scents worn by the nobles who were standing behind their chairs, waiting for the King's entrance.

The usher indicated my place, then took Lady Lucy farther down the table. The Ambassador's wife was shown to a seat on the other side, a little too far away for easy talk. As I glanced around I realized that almost everyone at this end of the table was speaking English; apparently it was the custom to seat the distinguished guests from each foreign country together. I would not, I was grateful to see, be marooned in the midst of the babble of rapid French that I could not yet follow with ease.

On each side of me were empty places. While I was wondering who would fill them, the same usher brought over a thin dark-haired young man and touched the chair on my right with his wand.

"*Ici, vôtre grâce,*" he said, then turned to me and bowed. "*La comtesse Ogle, je présente, s'il vous plâit, son grâce, le duc de Somerset.*"

I dipped in a curtsy; the Duke made a graceful leg; we exchanged shy smiles. I kept my eyes down, wondering what we would talk about at supper. The Duke of Somerset —a Seymour, of course. We were not related in any way, I was sure, nor had we met in London.

Now I saw that the usher was leading in a lady clad in a blue satin robe that made me hate my ugly black weeds even more. It was so artfully draped over her dimpled white shoulders and breast. Just the gown I had been longing for! Then I looked at her lovely face and my heart jumped into my throat. Was it possible?

It was. A rustle of satin skirts beside me, a whiff of familiar perfume, a soft voice gasping "Lisa!" and I was in my mother's arms.

After our quick embrace we stared at each other in wonder, both made tongue-tied by this unexpected encounter. It was three years since our last meeting, a short visit spoiled for us both by the chilly-eyed presence of my grandmother. Since then I had been wed and widowed and, with good reason, felt motherless and abandoned. But Lady Mary, by relating my mother's story, had made it possible for me to look at her today with understanding and love; and, as we now stood side by side, I had a sudden hope that I could, at last, turn to her for help.

A sound of trumpets, heralding the approach of King Louis XIV of France, silenced the chatter. Two guards and a *huissier* marched in first, followed by three officers of the royal kitchen. Next came a group of lackeys carrying hot food for the King's table, with a second pair of guards bringing up the rear. There had been a great poisoning scare the previous year, and Louis was taking no chances these days.

Now the trumpets pealed again and the King himself, preceded by the royal house steward and two ushers with flaming flambeaux, walked slowly to his high-backed throne chair at the high table.

I watched him with astonished eyes. Could this be the great Sun King, this sober, rather stout man in the dreary brown suit? I had seen portraits of him, painted when he was young and very handsome; now that he was in his forties, the aquiline nose was hooking toward a double chin and the full lips drooped peevishly.

And where, I asked myself, were the fabulous jewels, the priceless laces, the lavish satins and brocades? As far as I could see there was only a glint at his knees, a small twinkle of brilliants in his shoe buckles, and a few insignificant gems sewn into the rather greasy beaver hat—no rings, no orders, very little gold embroidery. He reached his place and faced the crowded salon, displaying a flash of a bright crimson needlework vest, but I did not feel that this made up for the plainness of the rest of his attire.

At this moment the young Duke of Somerset caught my eye. From the way he raised a surprised and amused brow at me, it seemed that Louis was not his idea of a great monarch, either. I smiled at him, suppressed a chuckle, and turned back to my mother. A quick shake of her head indicated that I must not speak, so I remained silent, wondering what would happen next.

While we all watched, King Louis sat down, took a linen napkin from the gold-enameled nef in front of him, and chose a gold knife and fork from the royal cadena. Then, apparently ready for his supper at last, he smiled around the salon at the rows of us still standing behind our chairs.

"*Mes amis,*" he said loudly, waving his hand, "*asseyez-vous, s'il vous plaît.*"

When the scraping of the chairs had subsided, the hum of conversation began again; food was passed, wine glasses filled, and more platters of hot meat were rushed in from the kitchens. A dozen noblemen were waiting on Louis, tasting everything he fancied before it touched his lips, and on either side of him sat France's highest ranking nobles—princes and princesses, all of royal blood.

I, however, was not interested in anyone but my mother, so incredibly *here*, sitting beside me at a table in the Louvre! It had crossed my mind that she might be in Paris, I knew she spent some of her time here, but until this evening I had had little hope that our paths would cross.

She, obviously, was as surprised as I was. "I cannot believe it," she said softly, taking my hand in hers under the lace-trimmed cloth. "My own Lisa, here in Paris! But why hadn't I heard? Where is Lady Percy? I don't see her."

"Home in England," I replied. "She sent me over with Lady Lucy—sitting there." I showed her where Lady Lucy was placed. "We arrived three weeks ago, but we've seen only the Ambassador and his lady. In fact, this is the first evening's pleasure we've had."

"Your grandmother's orders, I suppose. Tell me first where you are living—then why you are still in such heavy mourning. It seems unnecessary and most inappropriate."

"We have a set of pretty apartments on the Rue de Rivoli, overlooking the Tuileries gardens," I told her, then explained the reason for my somber attire. "Because she made me wear these weeds at Whitehall, I must now be consistent and wear them here."

"The same selfish, unfeeling woman she's always been!" My mother's voice was angry and bitter. "Making you conspicuous because she's quarreling with King Charles! And I'm unable to do anything about it—oh, Lisa, I've blamed myself so often, so often!"

"I don't mind these robes so much," I told her, "but I do need your help, Mother, and I need it now. I'm desperately unhappy—"

"You may be sure, my darling child, that I will do what I can. But we cannot talk here; the moment supper is over we'll slip away and find a private place to discuss matters. Watch me and follow me. Whatever you do, don't lose me in the crowd. And now we must talk to our other supper partners."

Turning obediently to the Duke of Somerset, I found him looking at me with interested, sympathetic eyes.

"Lady Montagu is my mother," I told him. "I did not know she was in Paris, and we were seated together just by chance."

"She's beautiful," he said, admiringly. "I wondered who she was when she came in."

I could see that he was rather puzzled, and for some reason I wanted to explain matters to him. I do not usually confide in strangers, but before I quite knew what was happening, I was telling him of my father's early death, my mother's remarriage, and my own marital experience.

"I thought you were very young to be wearing widow's weeds," he commented. "I know what it means to be forced into things at an early age—I became the Duke of Somerset at twenty when an angry Italian killed my older brother, and I'm still not accustomed to being called 'your grace'! I sometimes wish my parents had been simple yeomen, and I suspect you do, too."

Our talk became a bit more impersonal after that; he was making the Grand Tour, he told me, spending a year or two abroad as so many wealthy young noblemen do these days. "With," he added, "the usual tutor, chaplain, and body servants. I'm supposed to be learning languages and acquiring polish."

When the King rose and retired to his bedchamber, followed by a favored few—which did not include anyone at our table—I bade my young companion farewell and stayed close behind my mother through the slowly moving mass of lords and ladies. Although I was already intent on what I would tell *her*, I found myself hoping that someday Charles Seymour and I might meet again. He was so easy to talk to, so pleasant and understanding.

I caught up with my mother as she left the dining salon; taking my hand in hers, she whisked me swiftly through the antechamber, out a side entrance, and into a tiny empty retiring room. "We should have a good opportunity to talk here," she said. "Lady Lucy was in the center of a group of dawdlers when you and I made our way out of the salon.

"Now." She drew me down on a deep window seat. "Tell me why you are unhappy, Lisa, and what I may do to help you."

Plunging immediately into my story, I related everything that had happened to me, beginning with the day I encountered King Charles at Whitehall and ending with the day at Petworth when Grandam refused my hand to Carl.

"You could send for him, Mother," I went on eagerly, "send for him and arrange for us to be married here in France before my grandmother betroths me to someone else. There's no reason why I shouldn't wed Carl—he's rich, noble, a hero. What more can she want? After all, it was King Charles himself who presented Carl to me, and he said wonderful things about him."

I paused, suddenly realizing that my mother was looking distressed.

"Count Carl von Königsmark," she said slowly and thoughtfully, giving my lover his full title. "He's wellborn, of course, and very brave; I've heard of his heroic adventures. But"—and she now shook her head in a way that made my heart sink—"I've heard other tales, too, Lisa. Tales that I'm afraid make me agree with Lady Percy in this sorry business."

"Tales? What tales?" I asked instantly, my voice sharply insistent.

She hesitated, and I asked her again, even more sharply.

"I hate to hurt you, my dear, but the truth of the matter is that he might well make you miserably unhappy."

"Why? How?"

Reluctantly, my mother told me that my Carl was notorious for his feminine conquests, that he had broken hearts and ruined reputations in Sweden, that a shocking number of married women had succumbed to his charms in Spain, and that a lovely wellborn English girl had run away from her family and traveled all over Europe with him, disguised as his page. "She's in a convent here in Paris," she concluded hastily, "with his newly born daughter. He sends her money, I believe."

For a moment I could not speak; then I rose hotly to Carl's defense. "But most men of rank have amorous adventures," I said. "I've been told that we must shut our eyes to this sort of thing."

"Within reason, Lisa, yes. But Count Königsmark is only twenty-one, and to have such a—a history already is quite appalling. If you married, he would soon resume his ways."

"He loves me," I protested. "I will make him happy, so happy he won't ever look at anyone else!"

"That's what I told myself when I married your stepfather," she said sadly. "But his constant infidelities have made my life a misery."

Before I could think of any answer to *that*, Lady Lucy limped in. "So here you are, Lisa. I've been hunting and hunting—" She stopped, staring at my mother. "Why, Betty!"

"Yes, Lucy. Isn't it amazing? They placed me beside Lisa at supper, and I stole her away for a little talk. You know how seldom we meet." Rising, she walked to Lucy and kissed her warmly. "How are you, my dear? Join us." She indicated the cushioned seat, where there was more than enough room for three. "I have a favor to ask you."

"A favor?"

My mother smiled. "I would consider it a favor, Lucy. I want you and Lisa to come to me until I return to England. I'm alone this time, and we could be very happy together.

Lisa tells me you've been quiet here in Paris, and I would like to change all that. She should be meeting dozens of people and making new friends—particularly now."

"I quite agree," was Lady Lucy's reply. "But it can't be done. I must tell you frankly that Lady Percy has just learned that you are here, and I had a letter today ordering me to keep you and Lisa apart. In my opinion, Lisa should always have been in your care, but you know how I am placed—and if I don't obey those orders she'll be taken from me, too, and given a stricter chaperone."

"I know. Indeed, I know." My mother patted her thin shoulder and gave another heavy sigh. "I should never have married again, but it's too late now. Well, perhaps we can manage to meet 'by accident' here and there. . . ."

I returned to our apartments that night unhappier than ever, and I lay awake for hours, unable to sleep. What I had heard about Carl had, of course, hurt me deeply, and it took me a long time to convince myself, as I had tried to convince my mother, that Carl's past need not ruin our future together. He was so much handsomer than other men, so gay, so charming—naturally women would pursue him, and he was still too young to know how to avoid entanglements.

Marriage would change him.

❧

It rained heavily all the next day, and the next and the one after that. Looking out of a long window at the dismally dripping gardens laid out by King Louis sometime earlier, I wondered why everyone thought April a good month to be in Paris. Poor Lady Lucy, sniffling around in her bedchamber with a miserable cold in her nose, was no help in passing the hours, and when the sun finally broke through on the morning of the fourth day I was thoroughly bored and very restless.

"Let me take Dolly and walk in the gardens," I suggested. "You can't go out, I realize that, but I'll go mad if I stay in these rooms much longer. I'm not a prisoner, am I?"

"No," admitted Lucy, blowing her nose noisily, "Of course you're not. But I promised Lady Percy not to let you out of my sight here in Paris. I'm sure I don't have to tell you why."

"Well, you won't have to let me out of your sight. Here." I pulled a comfortable chair to one of the windows that overlooked the royal gardens. "Sit here. Dolly and I will stroll around under those chestnut trees, and you can watch us every minute."

"Do, my dear. Enjoy a little air and exercise. But before you leave me, I must tell you that I received another letter from your grandmother this morning. She's ordered us off to The Hague, where we are to stay with Lady Temple."

"Lady Temple?"

"The wife of Sir William Temple, who was our ambassador to Holland for so many years. You will like her, Lisa; she's charming, intelligent, gentle, and kind. She knows all there is to know about Holland, and she's a great friend of both Prince William and Princess Mary."

"She sounds much too nice to be a friend of Grandam's," I said.

"I believe they're merely acquaintances, but everyone stays with the Temples when they are strangers to Holland. She's quite accustomed to it."

I shrugged. "As far as I'm concerned, I will be glad to go to The Hague. Paris certainly has no charms for me—especially as I'm not allowed to see my mother."

A few minutes later, Dolly and I were safely inside the pretty pleasure gardens. I turned back and looked over at the gray stone building that housed our apartments. Yes, there was Lucy waving at me from the window.

The air today was sweet. The rains had freshened the streets, carrying off much of the refuse; the chestnut trees were loaded with fragrant candlelike blossoms; and the flower beds all around us were bursting with early spring flowers. My spirits rose, and I was actually smiling to myself when I noticed a tall young man who was crumbling some bread in his fingers and throwing it down for the pigeons.

He was wearing an unfashionable black peruke, a shabby coat of an odd foreign cut, and a wide hat that hid his face. But there was something about the way he held his head—

My heart leaped and began to pound. At that moment the man raised his head and looked directly at me. It was Carl.

I stopped so abruptly that Dolly almost climbed up my heels. Thinking rapidly, I gave a noticeable shiver and clutched my light cloak closer around my shoulders. "Dolly," I said, swinging around and facing my maid, "run and fetch me my warmer cloak. It's chillier than we thought."

"But milady—"

"Don't argue, Dolly, and stop shaking your head in that silly way. You won't be gone more than a minute or two, and I'll stay right in this very spot."

Still grumbling a little, she hurried away. I waited until she was out of earshot, then strolled a bit closer to where Carl was standing, tossing more bread to the pigeons. A dog frisked up to me; I bent over it and spoke as loudly as I dared.

"My cousin is watching me from the house over there. How did you find me?"

"I heard in London that you were in Paris, so I came and inquired at the British Embassy. How can we meet?"

"We can't. And we leave soon for The Hague."

"Then I'll follow you. Where will you stay there?"

"With Lady Temple."

"Good. It's small, The Hague. I will arrange a plan."

A quick glance across the Rue de Rivoli showed me Dolly, moving swiftly out of the house with my cloak over her arm. "I see my maid returning," I murmured, letting the little dog go.

Carl threw the last of his crumbs to the ground, dusted off his long fingers, and deliberately walked past me.

"I want you, *mitt hjärta*," he said, in a voice that sent a thrill through me. "Just remember—what I want I always get."

Our journey from Paris to The Hague was pleasant and uneventful. The weather was fine, the sea smooth, as we sailed up the coast, and the short overland drive from Maas showed me a countryside completely different from any I had seen in France or England. The flat green fields, broken here and there by patches of bright flowers, the fascinating windmills, their arms turning slowly in the light May breeze, and the narrow canals, empty except for an occasional barge—everything I saw delighted me.

It was late afternoon when we reached the outskirts of The Hague, and as we clattered over the brick-paved streets I feasted my eyes on the handsome houses and breathed in the fragrant air. Accustomed as I was to the stench in London and more recently in Paris, this neat little town seemed to me like a doll's village, made up of toy houses scrubbed daily and kept in careful order.

A turn, a few minutes later, took us into what was obviously the heart of The Hague: a charming lake dotted with snowy, drifting swans and bordered on two sides by imposing ancient buildings. Some had tall towers topped with sharp piercing spires; others had odd roof lines and gables. At one end of the decorative sheet of water stood a more modern group of houses, their stately façades trimmed with graceful stone garlands of fruit and flowers, their windows and roofs reminding me of the new London dwellings built to replace those razed by the Great Fire in 1666, some fifteen years ago.

Although I think I would have preferred one of the smaller, odder-looking houses, we pulled up in front of the newest and handsomest of them all, a large square building on the corner. But when I saw the beaming smile of welcome on the badly pock-marked face of Lady Temple, waiting to greet us, I forgot everything except how good it was to be with such a kind hostess. Later I learned that, although she was always very hospitable, she had a special reason for taking me into her home: the Temples' only daughter, Diana, had died when she was about my age, and Lady Temple had a warm spot in her heart for all young girls.

"My dear, dear child!" she said, kissing me on both cheeks. "And Lady Lucy Hay! How very happy I am to see you both. Come in, come in."

As she stepped back so we could enter, she clapped her hands, then addressed a stream of Dutch at three lackeys and two plump handmaids waiting for her orders.

"There," she announced. "The men will see to the coach and your boxes; Katje and Gretchen will show you to your rooms and help your women unpack. I know how weary you must be, so rest for an hour or so and I'll send up word when supper is ready. We will be quite alone this evening, which will give me an opportunity to tell you all about my dear Holland and its ways."

If the exterior of the house was a disappointment to me, the interior certainly was not. It delighted me. Instead of open hearths I saw large porcelain stoves standing on gaily tiled platforms; the walls were paneled in a much darker wood than we used in England and were more elaborately carved, and my bedstead was built right into one of them, so that I felt, when I climbed up into it, as if I were entering a cupboard. The only ornaments were bits of bright blue and white china, and the chattering Katje, practicing a few words in English, managed to convey that they had been made in a nearby town called Delft.

The room where we gathered for supper after our rest was much smaller than the dining halls at home and held only one long table, surrounded by heavy, intricately carved chairs. It was a single story high and there was no minstrels' gallery, but despite its low ceiling and the warm evening outside, it was cool, comfortable, and extremely inviting. Wide windows on two sides were open to catch the breeze, and before I took my seat beside Lady Temple I saw that there were pleasant views from all of them; the windows on the front overlooked the lake, the others opened on a large square.

"I hope," said Lady Temple, "that you will like this house as much as I do. When Sir William was ambassador here we lived at the Embassy, of course, and after a while it was home to us. So many years! But now that he has retired we have a house of our own at Sheen, on the Thames, and when we come back to Holland we let something convenient. This"—she waved her hand around the dining chamber—"is the loveliest house I have found so far. Nothing like your magnificent Petworth or Northumberland House, of course," she added, smiling at me, "but, for The Hague, unusually large and well planned.

"As you have probably already realized, life is very different here, much simpler and quieter than at home. Even the palace will strike you as small, and you will be quite surprised by the lack of ceremony. But"—and again she smiled at me—"one thing I *do* know, my dear, is that you and Princess Mary will be good friends. She is still very young and rather lonely here."

"I've heard she is not too happy," said Lady Lucy.

"No," replied Lady Temple a little hesitantly, "she is not. Nor too well. The climate disagrees with her, I'm sorry to say, and she suffers from attacks of ague. By the way"— she turned back to me—"you will find some kinswomen among the ladies of her suite. One of Lady Percy's sisters was Princess Mary's governess; she was born a Howard, of course, and married a Villiers. Three of her daughters came here with her Highness as ladies-in-waiting, and although one married a fine Hollander the other two still hold their posts."

She was too polite to mention what I had heard my grandmother discussing one day when she had apparently forgotten that I was in the room—that Betty Villiers, the oldest of the sisters, was the principal reason for Princess Mary's unhappiness. Prince William, or so she said, fell in love with Betty while he was in England courting Mary and succeeded in making her his mistress even before he and the Princess were married. It was their intimacy, which still continued, that cast a shadow on the royal union, despite the fact that Princess Mary was one of the few people unaware of the long liaison. He never loved her as she wanted him to, but she did not know why.

A note arrived from Princess Mary the following morning, inviting us all to the palace, so we ordered our chairs and made the short trip to the other side of the lake that same afternoon. The palace, built back in 1250, was a large Gothic building surrounded on three sides by a moat and, on the fourth, by the lake. It looked huge from the outside, but we discovered, as we trailed a royal servant to Mary's rooms, that the interior was made up of one dark, small, stuffy chamber after another. The Princess's apartments were no exception, and I thought them much less pretty and comfortable than those we occupied in Lady Temple's house.

Her Highness, when the usher announced us, was sitting listlessly in a chair by the window, a piece of needlework lying neglected in her lap. The moment we entered, she tossed the bit of linen aside, sprang to her feet, and stepped forward to greet us, her small face brightening.

Having seen several portraits of this niece of King Charles, I immediately decided that she was a great deal lovelier than her pictures. Silky dark curls hung almost to her slender waist, she had an unusually clear and white skin, and her dark eyes were an odd almond shape that added a charming insouciance to her expression.

"How good of you to come!" she said, including all three of us in her welcoming smile. "I've been longing for company—just yawning my way through the hours."

After Lady Temple had kissed her hand and presented us, Mary introduced Mistress Anne Villiers and Mistress Jane Worth, the only two ladies-in-waiting in attendance that afternoon, then led us all to a circle of chairs near hers.

"As you can see, we are most informal here," she said. "Do sit down and tell us all the latest news from London and Paris."

While I explained that I had had little opportunity to gather gossip in either city, I saw that the Princess was studying my face with as much interest as I had been studying hers. It seemed to me that there was compassion and understanding in the almond eyes that met mine, and I decided that Lady Temple had been right when she said that this lonely girl and I would soon be friends.

After an interval of general talk, our royal hostess suggested a game of basset, and Lady Temple, seeing that she was not needed to make up the table, slipped away home, telling Lady Lucy and me that our chairs would be waiting to take us back whenever we were ready.

Before long I realized that her Highness was an avid gambler, and I was glad that I knew the game well enough to make it interesting for her. Anne Villiers, whom I disliked at sight, kept slowing its progress by tracing our kinship on the Howard side, and Jane Worth, a small honey-haired girl with a sweet face, seemed to have her mind on something else. The fever of the game caught their interest after a while, however, and our five heads were bent intently over the cards when the door was suddenly flung open and a lackey announced his Highness.

Princess Mary, looking startled and a bit guilty, dropped her cards on the table. Before any of us could rise or leave the table, Prince William, followed by a taller and much handsomer gentleman, strode over to us. At best, I would describe his Highness's appearance as insignificant, and he apparently tried to make up for his lack of inches by adopting a stiff carriage and a stern, haughty, critical manner.

Sweeping all of us with a cold, disapproving frown, his frigid glance finally settled on his young wife.

"Frivoling away the day, as usual, madam?" he demanded. "I hoped to find you doing something more useful."

To my dismay, I saw Mary's lip quiver and her eyes fill with tears. She was trying to blink them back when the Prince spoke again.

"Won't you present your visitors? Manners, madam, manners!"

This second rebuke was too much for the Princess, and one of the tears escaped, slipping right down her cheek. Gulping back a sob, she made a blind gesture toward Lady Lucy and me. We were on our feet now, standing in a stricken silence, horribly embarrassed by the unpleasant scene.

To my great relief, the other gentleman bowed low and spoke for Princess Mary.

"As these two ladies are my cousins, your Highness," he said, "perhaps I might have that privilege." And with a pleasant smile, he moved to Lady Lucy and kissed her on the cheek.

"How long it has been, my dear Lucy, since we last met! Your Highness, may I present the Lady Lucy Hay?"

While Lucy was making her curtsy and kissing Prince William's hand, the stranger turned to me. "I am Harry Sidney," he explained. "My mother was Dorothy Percy, a sister of Lady Lucy's mother."

He then led me over to the Prince. "The Countess of Ogle, your Grace. Born Elizabeth Percy."

Although I was certainly bewildered to find the Dutch Court peopled with so many Howards and Percys, I saw that this particular kinsman was well worth having; when I later learned that he was a special envoy from King Charles to Prince William, I was not surprised. The ease, vivacity, and charm with which he had handled this awkward situation bespoke the true diplomat.

By the time William finished a polite speech of welcome and said he must return to his council chamber, Princess Mary had regained most of her composure. The Honorable Henry Sidney remained, chatting in a most comfortable fashion of many pleasant evenings the Princess and he had enjoyed together in the past.

When the color was back in her cheeks, he moved away and came over to me. "I was hoping to find you here," he told me, "as I bring you messages from our King. In a letter to me that arrived only a few hours ago, he bade me tell you how much he deplores your sudden mysterious disappearance from his Court after your first delightful meeting. He hopes for your early return and, in the meantime, he commands me to stand your friend in his place—one of the most welcome orders," he added warmly, "his Majesty has given me in many a long month."

His friendly manner made it easy to respond in kind; my usual shyness dropped away and, to my surprise, when he set us all laughing over an outrageous bit of gossip, I had the courage to venture a comment on the situation that set everyone off again. He was one of those rare people, apparently, whose own wit brings out an answering wit in others.

A striking clock reminded us that the afternoon was waning. Lady Lucy announced that we must return to Lady Temple, Harry asked for permission to see us to our chairs, and we thanked Princess Mary for a delightful visit.

"Call again tomorrow, please do!" she said to me as I bent over her thin fingers. "I would like very much to be your friend, Lady Ogle. I feel, somehow, that you and I have a great deal in common."

So began a lifelong friendship, doubly dear to me because it was my first with someone near my own age. Because Princess Mary and I met at a time when we both needed affection, understanding, and someone in whom to confide our troubles, this friendship grew swiftly, and although it was some weeks before we began exchanging secrets, I found myself spending most of my time with her at the palace within a very few days.

At first, of course, I waited with impatience for some word or message from Carl, rising each morning in high hopes that this would be the day, then seeking my bed at night in lowered spirits. But as time went on, and I was more occupied with her Highness, I made myself push my worries aside; Carl would find me soon, and in the meantime I determined to enjoy these peaceful hours.

One afternoon, as Princess Mary and I were sitting over our needlework, she told me that she and her ladies were preparing to move to the House in the Woods, a smaller, more comfortable palace situated in the country, about a mile from The Hague.

"It really belongs to William's Aunt Albertine Agnes," she said, "but we are free to use it as much as we want. It's charming, really charming; if I had my way I'd live there the year round. Beautiful rooms, lovely gardens, and remote enough to discourage casual visitors. Besides," she went on, her face lighting up, "there's a great painted chamber called the Orange Hall that's perfect for dancing. When I'm at the House in the Woods we dance almost every night. Don't you love dancing, Lisa? I do."

I fingered the skirt of my heavy black gown and sighed. "I think I would—I've really never had the opportunity to find out. I did enjoy my dancing lessons, but of course now these weeds bar me from such pleasure."

"Exactly when did Lord Ogle die?" asked Mary, leaning forward. She counted off the months on her fingers, after I replied, and gave a triumphant laugh. "I thought so. A year and a half this May. Why in heaven's name are you wearing them still?"

I flushed and explained.

"How ridiculous!" was Mary's instant comment. "I shall write Lady Percy and say so."

"Oh, no," I protested, a little frightened at the thought. "She'll make me wear them forever if you do that. It would just put her back up, your Highness."

"Not in the way I shall say it. Let me see—" and she went to her writing table and sat down.

"My dear Lady Percy," she said aloud while her pen glided over the paper. "I write to tell you how much I value Lady Ogle's company and to ask if you will allow her to discard her widow's weeds. I suffer greatly from the ague, a most dispiriting ailment, and I find that the sight of her black gown and veils adds to my melancholy. So give her permission to change to something more cheerful and please me, et cetera, et cetera." With a final flourish she signed the short note, scattered sand over the wet ink, and turned back to me.

"There! It will go to England with the next courier. And we won't wait for her answer. No"—when I again tried to protest, Mary raised her hand and silenced me—"I take full responsibility. I *command* you to throw away those ugly things!"

I laughed. "And appear in a morning gown? Or my shift?"

"You haven't any other Court robes?"

I shook my head. "Not with me. Grandam sent me off with only two of these for evening and afternoon. Another way of keeping me from enjoying myself."

"Well, in that case we will simply order you new gowns immediately. Not here; we must go to Amsterdam. Why not? I need a few new dresses myself." Her dark eyes began to shine, and she gave me an excited hug. "Perhaps Lady Temple will go with us—we'll take the royal barge and travel in comfort. I'll want Anne Trelawney, Mistress Langford, and Jane Worth." She sobered for a moment. "If a pleasure jaunt doesn't cheer Jane up, I shall have to ask her what's wrong."

To my great delight, Princess Mary's sudden scheme was acceptable to everyone concerned. When Lady Temple agreed to join our party, Prince William, who considered her a good influence on his wife, saw no reason why we should not go, and although I worried over the possibility of Carl arriving at The Hague during our absence I could not very well let that spoil a happy occasion.

Amsterdam, I knew, was only twenty-odd miles away, and we would not be gone more than a few days. I assured myself that Carl would either wait for me to return or ride to Amsterdam to find me. Then, having settled the matter in my mind, I climbed on board the gaily canopied barge with the rest of our party and proceded to enjoy every minute.

Our progress through the canals and up the Amstel River was leisurely and pleasant, and although we had cards and needlework with us we found we did not need them, preferring to sit idle under the awning, chatting easily together as we watched the vivid tulip fields, vine-covered houses, windmills, and lacy willow and alder trees drift by.

After our arrival there were, of course, certain formalities to be observed. The Stadholder's wife could not visit the city without being welcomed and fêted, and we had to dine with Burgomaster Valconier. He took us all to see the Stadhouse, the Court of the Admiralty, East India House, and Spein House for Old People—all, Mary said impatiently, a waste of a good day.

At her request, however, these interruptions were kept to a minimum. On the Sunday we sat through a two-hour sermon at the English church, but except for that we were free to spend the rest of our time poring over silks, satins, muslins, and embroidery patterns.

Princess Mary sometimes complained that our choice was too limited and longed for London shops and warehouses, but I was more than content with what we found in Amsterdam and with the city itself. The rows of tall red, green, or white houses with their varied gables and roof lines that edged the intricate web of canals were a source of constant interest to me, and I found myself wishing I could live in this clean, prosperous place and share the peaceful, bustling life of the wooden-shoed rosy-cheeked women.

But even as I dreamed of clattering to market each morning as they did and returning home with a basketful of eels, fish, cheese, and appetizing-looking vegetables and fruit for a fat husband's dinner, I ended by laughing aloud. For where would my handsome Count Carl, that adventurous gallant, fit into this placid picture?

I was standing at an open casement window, from which I could look directly across the canal into a room where a plump housewife was serving her lord and master with her own hands, when the absurdity of my dream struck me. Mary, entering the dark-paneled chamber at that moment, asked me what was so amusing.

"I have often wished the same thing," she said, after I explained. "If William and I could be truly alone I'm sure I could show him that I *do* love him, now. And he would have less to scold me about. It's trying to behave so primly at Court—that's almost impossible."

As it happened, no one else was with us, and in the uninterrupted hour that we then had together the young Princess bared her heart to me, telling me the whole sad story of her marriage. When King Charles ordered her to wed the stern Prince of Orange, Mary was deeply in love with a young Scottish nobleman. "I wept floods of tears," she said, "and I was still weeping on my wedding day. Then my beloved sister Anne caught the smallpox, and I had to leave England without even bidding her farewell. I was miserable for months—but I must confess that now I can barely remember my Scottish suitor's name, and I love William so much that I can hardly bear his cold indifference!"

Her ill health had made matters worse, of course, the ague and many miscarriages weakening her so that she could not control her tears whenever William criticized her behavior.

After she finished, I narrated my story. My early history was known to her, but the events that had followed my visit to Whitehall were not, and I took her fully into my confidence.

"The moment your Carl reaches The Hague," said Mary, apparently enthralled with my frustrated romance, "you must bring him to me, Lisa, and we'll think of a way to outwit your grandmother."

It was a cheering thought—although I had a few doubts that she could do it—and it was wonderful to have a young friend and confidante who saw no reason why Carl and I should not marry and live happily ever after. Another good result of our talk was that Mary, thinking Carl might already have arrived at The Hague, decided we should return there immediately.

"There's nothing to keep us in Amsterdam now," she said. "Your gowns are ordered, and I've made up my mind to send to England for that black raised satin."

Jane Worth, slipping in quietly a few minutes later, was sent off to arrange for the packing of our boxes.

"What can be wrong with her?" asked Mary after the girl left us "She is so changed, Lisa. She used to be the merriest of my ladies—dancing and singing all the time, laughing, joking. I hardly know her now, with her red eyes and headaches."

"Could she be in love, too?"

"I've thought of that, of course, and I think it must be the answer. Count Zulestein, a kinsman of William's, was very attentive to her some months ago—born on the wrong side of the blanket, but a great favorite of my lord's. It seemed to come to nothing, and it might well be that she's breaking her heart over him."

∽❧∾

There was still no sign of Carl when we returned to The Hague, and, as Mary was too occupied in moving her household to the House in the Woods to need my company, I found myself idle and bored. I was dawdling around my chamber, late one afternoon, watching a fair that had been set up in the square below our windows; rows of booths were filled with things to buy and games to play, small platforms had been erected for wrestling matches and other feats of physical prowess, and the townspeople were beginning to gather.

Off to the far side of the square, lined up in front of small tents, I saw a company of soldiers being drilled by a stout officer in a bright uniform, his shouted orders ringing like pistol shots through the laughter and talk of the crowd. While I was still there at the window a handsome coach, richly painted and decorated with a gilded coat of arms, rolled up and halted. Out stepped a gentleman, a tall cane in one hand, who handed down a masked lady. To my surprise, her gown was plain. A moment later a second coach arrived, pulled up beside the first, its occupants joined the others, and all four mingled with the townspeople.

I soon lost sight of them. A band of musicians, almost directly under my casement, struck up a lively dance, my feet moved to the beat, and I laughed aloud.

Lady Temple, entering, laughed with me and handed me

a mask. "Your cousin Harry and six other gentlemen have come to take us to the fair," she said. "If we go now I see no reason why we should not enjoy it. Later, it may be too rowdy. The pickpockets won't be at work yet, nor have the soldiers had time to become drunk."

"Pickpockets and soldiers?" Lady Lucy, joining us, protested. "Wouldn't it be wiser for Lisa to remain here and watch from the window? Lady Percy—"

"Oh, forget. Lady Percy for one evening! Harry has brought three young men from the Embassy, all of whom I know well; Mynheer Van Ghent, an old friend; and two tall noblemen from Sweden, two brothers named von Löwenhaupt. If they can't take care of us we must be helpless indeed. We're plainly dressed, and we'll carry no money."

If Lady Lucy replied, I did not hear her. I was suddenly filled with a wild flood of hope. I followed Lady Temple downstairs and into the room where my cousin and his friends were waiting. My eyes moved from one strange face to another—and yes, there he was, his blue eyes meeting mine, his golden hair sweeping his collar.

The fair was in full swing and the square so packed with merrymakers that there was no problem in mingling with them unnoticed. Ours were by no means the only masks in evidence; it seemed to me that every high-ranking lady within fifty miles of The Hague must be there, her face hidden, as was mine, behind a little oval of black muslin.

At Lady Temple's suggestion we divided our unwieldy company of nine into three groups, which gave each woman two escorts. "And remember," she cautioned us, "go back to the house at the first sign of rowdiness. Supper will await our convenience."

How Carl managed to be one of my little party I do not know. How he contrived to steal me away from Harry, my other gallant, was quite simple: after watching a wrestling match for a few minutes, the three of us had pushed our way through the jostling, laughing mob until we reached one of the shooting galleries. The moment it was Harry's turn to try his skill, when his eyes were glued to the target and the gun was resting on his shoulder, Carl jerked me instantly out of sight behind him and then off into the thickest of the crowd.

Paying not the slightest attention to my laughing protest, he wove a zigzag course to a sheltered spot near Lady Temple's house.

"Now," he told me triumphantly, "the good cousin will search for us in that melee, and here we will be, waiting for him like two good children. But the next few minutes, my heart, are mine." And without giving me time to say a word he pulled me behind an empty wagon and took me in his arms.

After too short a time, we retraced our steps to a spot where Harry could find us. While I tucked my hair into place under my hood and retied my mask, Carl recounted some of his adventures since our unsatisfactory meeting in Paris.

"I set out to find von Löwenhaupt," he told me, "to persuade him to come here with me. He's my sister Amelia's husband, you see, and I can call him brother. I helped him when he was courting *her*, so I knew he would help me. And he agreed; he joined me the moment I caught up with him in Brussels, and here we are. Finding him was what took me so long."

In my turn I told him about my visit to Amsterdam and Princess Mary's offer to play matchmaker.

"It is good of her," replied Carl slowly, thoughtfully. "And perhaps we will take advantage of her kindness. I think it might be wise, however, for me to call myself von Löwenhaupt for a while. Prince William might object to her meddling in such a matter, and a careless word of hers could spoil everything. So don't tell her yet, Lisa—this way we will meet openly until I know whether or not I can arrange our marriage myself." Stopping suddenly, he waved over the heads of some soldiers standing near us. "Here comes the cousin. Ah, he sees us now."

I laughed to myself at how convincing Carl sounded as he acted out his story to Harry Sidney. The great press of people that separated us at the shooting gallery, our futile search for him, and our final decision to wait by the wall of Lady Temple's house—I almost believed it, it was so detailed.

It did seem to me that Harry's eyes were twinkling at me while he listened, but all he said was that, as all had ended well, it might be better not to mention the matter to Lady Lucy or Lady Temple.

❧

We were invited to the House in the Woods the following afternoon. As our carriage drove up the avenue bordered with tall trees, I wondered whether I would be able to keep my secret from Mary. What would I do if she asked me whether Carl had arrived in town during our absence? Should I have to lie?

Not knowing the answer, I put the problem out of my mind as best I could and watched with interest for our first glimpse of her Highness's favorite palace. The moment it came in sight I knew why she loved it so much. It was, certainly, a most charming building, and on this sunny May morning it could not have been more inviting. The graceful little flight of stone steps, the long windows, the beautiful fanlights, the tray-shaped roof with its fascinating dome— everything I saw enchanted me.

While we waited for Mary's usher, I stood looking first at the handsome marble floor and the pair of staircases arching over a double doorway that apparently led into the palace itself, and then at the delicate ironwork, the ornamental garlands of fruit and flowers, and many other pretty details that made me wish this little place belonged to me.

We found our young hostess sitting in one of the salons that opened into the gardens at the rear, a room as different from her chambers in the old town residence as day is from night. Here sunlight streamed in through several floor-length windows, and high ceilings and pale walls made it appear even more spacious than it was; and it seemed to be a perfect background for the dark-eyed English princess.

Mary jumped up and gave us a hearty unroyal hug.

"We're settled at last," she said happily. "Isn't it lovely here? I couldn't wait any longer to show it to you!"

She pulled me over to a window and pointed out other things for me to admire—a maze, a pretty little pavilion, bright flower beds and masses of early blossoming shrubs. We were still gazing at the enchanting pleasure grounds when Jane Worth entered the room, followed by two heavily laden tiring women.

"Yes," said Mary, laughing at my gasp of joy, "here are our gowns. They arrived this very morning."

"Already?" I could hardly believe it. "Oh, let me see them, let me touch them!"

Everyone laughed, and for the next hour we ceased to be a royal princess, a fifteen-year-old widowed countess, an unhappy maid-in-waiting, and an elderly ambassador's wife, and were simply four women reveling over gleaming armfuls of satin, muslin, ribbon, and lace.

"We'll dance tonight," announced Mary firmly as she watched me caressing a silver robe laced down the front with delicious mauve ribbons. "To tell you the truth, Lisa, the moment I heard our gowns were here I ordered the musicians to be ready and sent word to Harry Sidney to bring us some dancing partners. He loves to dance himself, and we can trust him to find us the handsomest and nimblest of our foreign visitors."

My pulse quickened. Carl would surely be one of our party this evening; we would dance together for the first time, and I would wear the silver gown.

"Let me keep Lisa here," suggested Mary to Lady Temple. "Or, better still, both of you spend the night with us. We may want to dance late."

Lady Temple shook her gray curls. "I've letters to finish that must go off tomorrow morning, but I'll send Lady Lucy back with Lisa's tiring woman and everything she'll need for the night."

Mary and I went for a stroll in the garden after Lady Temple returned to The Hague, and when we were far enough from her ladies to talk privately she told me she had discovered what was wrong with Jane Worth.

"You were right, Lisa. She *is* in love, and it *is* Count Zulestein. It seems that he seduced the poor child after promising to marry her. Oh, he meant it at the time and would still like to, but William has persuaded him that he should look higher for a wife. That royal blood of Zulestein's! Ridiculous, of course, but that's William for you. And I can't be angry with Jane—she thinks she's disgraced herself and me and talks of suicide."

When I asked if Prince William might not change his mind, Mary said no. "Once he says anything it's like the laws of the Medes and Persians. No, we'll wait until William goes off some place and wed them secretly. My almoner, my dear Dr. Kenn, you know, has promised to help us."

"Perhaps I could be a witness," I said. "Or am I too young?"

Neither of us knew; in fact, we were both woefully ignorant on the subject of marriage laws. "We'll leave it all to Dr. Kenn," Mary decided, and we joined the others.

Later, as I was about to change for the evening, Mary, already dressed, came to my chamber. "I want to see you stripped of these crow feathers," she told me, her eyes dancing with such delight that I found it hard to believe she was five years my senior and a married woman. She had said that William rarely came to the House in the Woods, and never without warning, and it was possible that here, free of his frowns and scoldings, she felt like a girl again.

Now she sat and watched while Dolly removed my widow's coif and veil and unbuttoned my black high-necked gown. As I stepped out of the heavy garment I wrinkled my nose in distaste. No matter how much cinnamon Dolly had rubbed into it, it still smelled musty from so much constant wear in warm weather, and I gave it a little kick before she could pick it up and carry it away.

She returned with a silver basin of water, heavily scented because all the water in Holland was stored underground and had an unpleasant odor, and sponged my arms, shoulders, and neck, dried them with a soft linen towel, then unloosed my hair.

As it fell to my waist, Mary gave a gasp and her almond eyes opened wide.

"Your hair Lisa! How beautiful it is! I had no idea."

"I hate it!" I answered savagely. "They call me 'Countess Carrots' in London. How would you like that? You'd be 'Princess Carrots,' of course."

Mary gurgled with laughter. " 'Countess Carrots'—I don't think I'd mind, Lisa. It's amusing."

While we talked, Dolly laced me into my corset and tied on a fresh petticoat; then she helped me step into the full-skirted underdress that came with the silvery gown and, finally, the shining, glowing robe itself, with its bow-trimmed bodice and heavily ruffled sleeves.

Mary sighed contentedly. "Ravishing," she said. "Absolutely ravishing. The bows are perfection. Now, will you dress your hair à la Fontanges with some of that mauve velvet ribbon, or in curls like mine?"

Dolly reached for a brush and swept my hair back off my forehead. "I think, your Highness," she ventured, "that my lady looks her loveliest with it smooth—see, like this—a ribbon bow holding it at the back, and just the ends brushed into a row of ringlets." Her fingers were busy as she explained. "We've tried the other styles, arranging it over a French wire frame and covering her forehead with clusters of curls, but it was all wrong."

When Dolly was finished, Mary agreed. "Add a black taffeta patch there at the corner of her mouth, and she will be quite perfect." She rose and started for the door. "By the way," she said, "William's nicest aunt, the Princess of Oost Friesland, has arrived, bringing with her two young men to dance with us, her son Cornelius and the Duke of Somerset."

"The Duke of Somerset!" I exclaimed. "Oh, you will like him—he's young, pleasant, very easy to talk to. I met him in Paris, at the Louvre."

"Wasn't there some scandalous story about his older brother? Didn't some Italian shoot him because he insulted his wife?"

"It's possible. He did say his brother was dead but I never heard what happened. But if it is true, the present Duke is most unlike his brother. I can't imagine him insulting anyone."

❧

The evening, one I will never forget, began with an informal reception in the charming salon where Mary and I had spent our afternoon. The Princess of Oost Friesland, who was living in the dower house of the little palace, a house called the Old Court, was a stout, square, agreeable lady, and her son was a younger version of herself. I was presented to them first. As I swept down in one of my deepest curtsies to the older woman, it seemed to me she was looking at me in an odd, calculating manner.

I soon forgot it, however, for my eyes, a moment later, met those of Charles Seymour, standing behind the plump Dutch noblewoman. I remembered them as gray-blue, gentle and friendly; tonight they seemed darker, and I thought I saw a glint of startled admiration and perhaps something even warmer. I know I blushed and dropped mine immediately.

Then, before I had quite regained my composure, Carl was ushered into the room, and as he bowed over my hand he whispered the same word Mary had used earlier: "Ravishing!" That was all, but it was enough to flood my cheeks with color again.

I'm afraid the color was still there when Harry Sidney took Carl's place to greet me, and he smiled in such a knowing, quizzical manner that I grew a little frightened. Had he learned Carl's real name—and would he tell Lady Lucy?

I was still worrying about it during supper, but by the time we gathered in the Orange Hall to begin our evening's pleasure I had put it out of my mind. While I waited with Lady Lucy on one side of the oddly shaped, domed chamber, I studied the walls, every inch of which were covered with vast murals depicting the life of William's grandfather, Prince Frederick Henry. The four deep bays, the ceiling—everything was elaborately decorated; even the floor, at which I finally looked to rest my dazzled eyes, was laid out in a dizzying pattern of contrasting woods.

It was a relief when the music began and Mary rose from

her chair and danced the opening measures of a stately pavane with the Dutch Prince. A moment later her dwarf page brought the Duke of Somerset to me as a partner. As the highest-ranking visitors, we were expected to join the royal couple on the floor.

Having danced only with my dancing masters at Pet-worth, I was very nervous at first, but Charles Seymour proved to be such a skillful dancer that this soon passed and I forgot that there were just four of us performing. Another couple appeared before long, then another, and when the music stopped I was eager to begin again.

This time Prince Cornelius partnered me, and as it was a romping Dutch country dance, much like our English dances, I enjoyed it thoroughly, dipping, twisting, twirling with the best of them. I know I was laughing and panting when I returned to Lady Lucy, and I had to pat my hair into place and straighten my gown.

Carl now moved swiftly to my side and claimed the next one, murmuring under his breath to me while we were taking our places. "The gown is enchanting," he whispered. "I fall in love all over again! My small Countess Carrots is a dream come true tonight."

He caressed the name with his voice and me with his eyes. I discovered that I no longer hated my nickname, and a curious sense of exhilaration came over me as I matched my steps to Carl's in a fast and energetic coranto.

My heart sang with joy. I was dancing with my lover, among new and dear friends, pleasant acquaintances, and protective kinspeople.

Princess Mary, little Jane Worth, Charles Seymour, my cousins Lucy and Harry—most of them had problems, as I did. But they were here, enjoying the evening, and the haunting loneliness I had known for so long fell away and something warmer took its place.

I'm not merely Lady Percy's granddaughter, I told myself. I'm the Countess Ogle—yes, I'm Countess Carrots. *She's* not even a true Percy. I am, and I will not allow that cruel old woman to ruin my life!

8

The next few days passed so pleasantly that I found myself
wishing I need never leave Holland and my dear Mary. She
continued to be happy and gay; Carl, Charles Seymour,
and Harry Sidney were constant visitors whenever I was at
the House in the Woods, and although I rarely had more
than a minute or two alone with Carl he always made me
feel that it would not be long before our problem would be
solved. His attitude was possessive, assured, firm.

Early in June Mary learned that her lord was off to
Amsterdam for a week, and soon after his departure I received an urgent summons to join her next morning. To my
surprise, I was taken directly to her chapel.

There, with even greater surprise, I found not only
Princess Mary waiting for me; the small chamber seemed
full of familiar faces—Jane Worth, Count Zulestein, Dr.
Kenn, and Carl. There was only one stranger, a young
Frenchman I had met briefly at an embassy party. As Mary

came to greet me, I realized, before she spoke, why we were all here.

"Dr. Kenn has agreed to marry Jane and Count Zulestein," she told me, "and except for you I have asked only foreign friends to witness the ceremony. If William is angry, and he may well be, he cannot punish *them*. Come, Lisa, we are ready to begin."

The service, which Dr. Kenn performed in English, sounded beautiful to me that day, probably because of the happiness on Jane's face. Whatever reluctance her bridegroom might have had now seemed dispelled; he held her hand closely and spoke his responses as a man should, and my eyes, meeting Carl's, filled with tears. One morning soon, I thought, we two might stand together and say these same words.

Almost before it seemed possible, the ceremony was over, Jane and Count Zulestein were man and wife, and Dr. Kenn was asking for witnesses to sign the marriage papers. Carl, who apparently had not known why he was invited to be present, suddenly looked extremely disturbed. Then, realizing that he could not refuse, shrugged his shoulders slightly and, in his turn, scrawled something on the paper.

Mary, glancing down at the signatures, stared at him in amazement, then at me, widening her eyes. Dr. Kenn, however, handed it to Count Zulestein without examining it further, and he put it in one of his deep coat pockets.

As we all crowded around the young couple, Princess Mary warned us that the wedding must, for a while, be kept secret. "Until the Count and his Countess have informed their families," she added, smiling at them. "And now I will take Lady Ogle to the garden. Suppose you join us there in a moment or two, as you would if you were making a morning call."

What her household thought, I don't know. Mary told me that she had sent her other ladies into The Hague for several hours so they would have no responsibility in the business. Then, leading the way to the pavilion, she patted the seat beside her and bade me sit down.

"Now," she ordered, "tell me just why you deceived me about your Carl. Did he think I could not be trusted to keep a secret?"

"I wanted to bring him to you immediately," I replied, "but he was afraid Prince William might not want you involved in his schemes. He thought it best to use the name von Löwenhaupt until he has arranged a way for *us* to wed."

"If I'd known, I would not have asked him to be a witness to Jane's ceremony. He had to sign his real name, of course. Well, it can't be helped now; I'll tell Count Zulestein there is a good reason for his deception, and no one else need know. In the meantime, Lisa, I will try to think of some way to help you."

She managed, a little later, to have a private talk with Carl and me, asking him right out why he did not arrange a secret ceremony here in Holland and take me away to Sweden.

"I must first make sure, your Highness," he answered, "that Lady Percy could not annul our marriage. Lisa is not yet of age, you know."

"Would it matter, if you were in Sweden? She couldn't take Lisa from you."

"No, but she could hold all the Percy inheritance."

"Let her!" I said. "I want to be happy, Carl, not rich."

"So you think now, my heart. But later you might be sorry and blame me. Not for yourself, perhaps, but for your children." He smiled tenderly at me as he spoke; then he looked off into space and his face hardened. "I think your grandmother would like to have that happen and keep the money—but she will not defeat me so easily! All will be as it should be. We shall have each other and everything that is truly yours."

Mary said nothing more, then or later when we had a moment alone, and after I retired that night and thought back over the conversation, I became increasingly disturbed. Was I a stupid little fool to think Carl loved me? Was it not more likely that he, too, wanted my huge fortune? After all the beautiful women who had thrown themselves into his arms, why would he fall in love with *me*, young, awkward, redheaded?

I lay awake for hours, torturing myself. The same thoughts continued to haunt me all the next day, which I spent quietly with Lady Temple, and were still on my mind when Lady Lucy and I visited Princess Mary the following afternoon. The three of us were sitting with our needlework, chatting quietly. I don't remember where the other ladies were, but just as I was rethreading my needle the door into the salon was thrown open and Prince William, alone and unannounced, strode in.

One glance at his stormy face told me why he was there, and his first words proved I was right. Before we could rise, he reached Mary's side and began shouting at her.

"How dared you do it, madam, how *dared* you do it? You knew I'd forbidden Zulestein to marry that wanton of yours, but the very moment my back was turned you *dared*—"

He was almost incoherent, and I could see that Mary had begun to shake.

"Jane is not a wanton, my lord," she protested courageously, somehow holding back her tears. "Count Zulestein seduced her with promises of marriage, which he was quite willing to keep after Dr. Kenn discussed the matter with him."

"Ah, Dr. Kenn! I have him to thank for this, have I? And where is that meddling fool?"

"Right here, your Highness." Dr. Kenn entered, apparently brought in from the adjoining room by William's raging voice.

The Prince swung around and faced him, looking even blacker than before. "Well, I will tell you, as you are the guilty party, that I shall have this marriage annulled."

"I think not, sir." Dr. Kenn's voice was gentle but firm. "The young couple are of age, and I was careful to perform the ceremony in accordance with man's law as well as God's. I will defend it in open court, if necessary."

"You traitorous, sneaking Englishman—" William's hand rose as if to strike Mary's chaplain, and he took a step nearer the small, swarthy cleric.

"Thank God I am an Englishman! You have no authority over me, and I need not suffer your insults." Dr. Kenn crossed to Mary, who could barely stand. "With your permission, my dear lady, I shall return home on the first packet."

Mary burst into violent sobs. "No, no—do not desert me! I need you, dear sir! I need you!" She fell into her chair and covered her face with her hands, weeping uncontrollably. I was alarmed. I ran to her and tried to calm her, and Lady Lucy limped over to us, a vinaigrette in her fingers.

"Loosen her gown," she said. "Sniff this, your Highness."

But Mary pushed it away, her sobs rising. The door opened again and in rushed Mistress Langford, Mary's old nurse.

"Call the physician," said Lady Lucy.

"It's the ague." Mistress Langford knelt and took Mary in her arms, murmuring softly. I moved away and saw, to my relief, that Prince William looked rather ashamed and a little worried.

"I hope, sir," he said stiffly to Dr. Kenn, "that you will not be hasty. If I offended you, remember that I had good reason for my anger."

Dr. Kenn bowed distantly and made no reply.

William flushed, took a step toward the door, then, as Mary burst into fresh sobs, halted.

"It—it isn't the ague," she all but screamed to her nurse. "Dr. Kenn is—is leaving me!"

The Prince, looking really frightened now, spoke again. "I apologize, Dr. Kenn. For the Princess's sake, please forgive my remarks and remain with her."

Mary now pulled away from Mistress Langford and added her pleas to his, begging Dr. Kenn to stay for at least another year. He must promise her that.

It was such a painful scene that we were all thankful when the cleric finally gave the hysterical Princess the pledge she wanted, and soon the physician arrived, making it possible for us to leave the little palace.

I was so exhausted that I ate lightly, planning to retire early. Before we rose from the table, however, a lackey brought in Harry Sidney.

"A letter came for you, Lucy," he said, "in a bag of mail that arrived at the Embassy. It's marked urgent."

I saw the Percy lion on the seal, as he handed it to my cousin, and my heart sank. Any letter from my grandmother did this to me.

She tore it open, read a few lines, and gave a gasp.

"What is it now?" I asked.

"We're to come home. No reason given, of course. The Percy yacht is waiting for us at Maeslandsluys to take us directly to Alnwick, where Lady Percy will meet us. We're not to delay a day."

While I sat stricken, Harry reached for the letter and read it himself. "A strange woman," he said. "Would she mind if I traveled with you? I have a letter, too. Mine is from the King, recalling me to England."

"Land ho!" A shout from the crow's nest took me swiftly out on deck and over to the rail. On the horizon lay a dark, irregular line; as further proof that we were nearing land, I saw several sea gulls circling our yacht, screaming like infants deprived of their milk.

For a long moment I stood there alone, wondering what new trial awaited me in England. And what had Carl done when he learned of my unexpected, inexplicable departure? Set out for England, or given me up for lost?

There had been no way to see him again; all I could do, in the flurry before leaving The Hague, was to enclose a letter in the farewell note I sent Princess Mary. Her reply, which reached me as Lady Lucy and I were kissing Lady Temple good-bye, said she would deliver my message. She added that I would always be welcome at her Court—to come to her whenever I could.

Whenever I could! The phrase echoed hollowly in my

despairing heart. Would I ever see my dear friend or Holland or my lover again?

The coast line dimmed as tears filled my eyes. Hearing footsteps behind me, I wiped them quickly away. It was my cousin, Harry Sidney, who had made the sea crossing with us. For a few minutes we stood in silence; then he looked down and smiled into my face.

"As this may be our one opportunity to talk in private, Lisa," he said, "there is something you and I should discuss."

I glanced up, surprised.

He laughed. "Now come, my dear child—you must know what I mean! Lucy may have been blind to a certain Swedish masquerade back in The Hague, but I assure you I was not. I knew that one reason you had been sent away was the handsome and dashing young Count Carl von Königsmark, so I was not too astonished to meet a 'Carl von Löwenhaupt' traveling with the husband of Königsmark's sister."

"I *did* think you suspected us, but when you said nothing I was sure I was wrong. Promise me you won't tell my grandmother, Cousin Harry—I'm miserable enough without that!" My voice shook.

"Of course I won't, silly chit! But there is someone else who will soon be asking me questions about you, Lisa, and that is King Charles. Shall I say you wish to marry Königsmark and need his help?"

I thought that over as swiftly as I could, realizing that all my doubts about Carl were foolish. This might well be my only chance to reach his Majesty's ear, and I realized that the message I sent him might change the course of my life.

"Say I am in desperate need of his help and friendship," I began. "Tell him I will wed Carl or no one, and that I shall defy my grandmother if she has arranged another marriage for me. Beg him to protect me, Harry—you know Grandam."

He nodded. "I do. And I will not forget what you have said. I would help you myself if I could—but Lady Percy *is* your guardian, and I can only be your courier. Let me know, when you can, what the old dragon is up to!"

⟋⟍

When we landed at Alnmouth the innkeeper there was quite ready to provide us with horses for the six-mile ride to the castle, saying that it was not often his privilege to serve a Percy. We mounted, and as we turned inland, leaving behind the dunes, the soft green sea moss, and the blue waters, I began to feel like a prisoner returning to jail; and the first sight of Alnwick's ancient battlements, topped with tall stone warriors set up to frighten off the foe back in 1350, almost made me ill.

Only too soon we reached the drawbridge, passed through the time-darkened barbican gateway, and clattered into the keep court. Stableboys ran to help us off our horses, the state entrance was thrown open, and Havering, our chamberlain, bowed his welcome. Lady Percy, he told us, was in the banqueting hall.

As we followed him it struck me, perhaps for the first time, what a bleak place my Alnwick Castle was. It was built to quarter soldiers and, in 1514, had once housed over three thousand men. We so rarely used it as a residence that my grandmother always found it necessary to bring many of her staff with her as well as several wagon loads of household goods. What furnishings there were had been made for the castle in the reign of Queen Elizabeth—heavy tables, chairs, court cupboards, and curtained beds.

The tapestries on the stone walls looked as if they had been hung when the place was first built, very few of the floors were covered by carpets, and although it was now July fires were burning brightly and the wind, when we climbed up into one of the towers, howled around the stone walls.

As we trailed Havering through echoing guardrooms and a string of empty little antechambers, Harry and I exchanged wry smiles. Lady Lucy, completely exhausted from days of seasickness and her ride, had fallen behind.

"It's been years since I was last here," said Harry. "I'd forgotten that you walk miles before you reach the habitable part."

"Grandam brought me here four years ago," I replied. "What I best remember are the stone figures, the wild winds, the heavy bedclothes at night, and my fear of ghosts."

Harry laughed. "I never worried about ghosts," he said. "I was too busy picturing Hotspur and his knights, drinking and feasting, struggling in and out of all that creaking armor"—he waved a hand at a suit standing rusty and neglected in a corner—"and then riding blithely over the moors to fight the Douglas at Otterburn."

We said nothing more; we were approaching the banqueting hall, and before we crossed its threshold our ears were assaulted by Lady Percy's strident tones issuing a series of imperious rebukes to some hapless underling.

I shivered, clutching at my ebbing courage. Must I always turn into a frightened child at the sound of that voice? No, I told myself fiercely, I would not! From now on *I would not!*

With this resolve in mind I faced my grandmother haughtily, my head high and my curtsy stiffly formal.

She stared at me in surprise, then gave a sneering laugh. "Court manners, Elizabeth? I see you are quite the great lady now!"

Without any further word of welcome she waved me aside and extended her glittering fingers to my cousin.

"This is a surprise, Harry. Where did you spring from?"

"If you must know," he answered, giving her his most ingratiating smile, "I have been taking advantage of your hospitality. My orders to return home arrived in Holland when Lisa and Lucy were about to set sail, and I had the presumption to come along with them. Uninvited, as you see."

"Don't be ridiculous, Harry," said my grandmother brusquely. "I'm grateful that they had your company and protection. We both know you could have made the journey in half the time by sailing directly to London."

As I expected, I had no private conversation with my guardian until after Harry left us. Even then she made me wait, and I decided that she was delaying on purpose, playing her cat-and-mouse game to make me uneasy and subservient. But this time, no matter how long she kept me guessing, her scheme would not work.

Summoned at last, I walked into her room, quietly and— on the surface, at least—calmly prepared for the worst.

"Lucy tells me," she began, with an affability that did not fool me for one minute, "that you had a very gay time in Holland. Buying new gowns, dancing half the night, and living in Princess Mary's pocket."

"Her Highness was extremely kind."

"Another pleasure-loving Stuart. They're all the same. However"—and there was something about the way she said the word that made me hide a shiver—"I am glad you enjoyed yourself. You've had a carefree holiday, and now we will talk seriously about your future."

"Until you give me permission to marry Carl, there is nothing to talk about."

"Still mooning over that fortune-hunting Swede? I would be doing you no kindness, Lisa, in giving you that permission! Instead—and for this you will thank me someday —I have arranged for you to wed a suitable gentleman of great wealth, a husband with whom you can be happy if you choose." Her eyes on me, she leaned back in her chair and straightened her skirts. "The settlements are being drawn up at this very moment, and a few more weeks will see you at the altar."

"A few more weeks may see me at the altar," I replied hotly, "but they won't see me wed! You can drag me there —you have more than enough lackeys for that. Do it, by all means. But I warn you, madam, that I'll be kicking and screaming every inch of the way. And if your clergyman is still willing to perform the ceremony after that, he will find that there is no power on earth that will make me take the wedding vows!"

To my surprise, I discovered that I was actually enjoying myself. I watched my grandmother's face growing more and more enraged, and when it was a deep purple I walked over to a chair and sat down.

"Get up! Get up!" She was almost shouting. "How *dare* you sit in my presence without my permission?"

I shrugged and looked her right in the eyes. "From now on I dare do many things. You forget that I am a countess, too, thanks to you. So why should I not sit? If it offends you, madam, try to make me leave this chair. Why not? It would be excellent practice for dragging me to the altar."

For the first time in my memory, my grandmother was

speechless. She rose to her feet and swept to the door. When she reached it she turned to glare at me.

"I will be your guardian for six more years, Elizabeth. How would you like to spend them all here at Alnwick?"

"His Majesty might have something to say about that."

"And send an army up to rescue you, perhaps? Or throw me into the Tower? Because you are in ill health and need the quiet I can give you here? Don't try my patience too far, I warn you! I leave here in a se'nnight. Until then you shall remain in your rooms and make up your mind to obey me."

❧

The day of Lady Percy's departure rolled around, and she came to my chamber. My boxes were packed but I was standing there in my chamber gown.

"Still acting the fool, Elizabeth? You have an hour to ready yourself for the journey."

"Not if it means marrying anyone but Carl."

"Oh, God, what a young idiot! All right—try living here and see how you like it. I'll send for you when you decide to behave!"

10

July ended and August brought us a spell of clear, sunny weather, days that lured me out of my dismal quarters and into the meadows below the castle. In accordance with my grandmother's orders I was allowed to walk, accompanied by a lackey, through the sally port and down the hillside as far as the Lion Bridge; but not even with Lady Lucy could I go over the drawbridge and into the town of Alnwick. Even through Grandam had confiscated all my money, she was taking no chance of my finding some way to send a message to the King.

If I had not been so unhappy I might have enjoyed rambling up and down the steep slope, so thickly covered with fir, beech, and silvery birch trees. The sun was warm, the needles underfoot soft and fragrant; but the light breeze, when it came from the east, carried a hint of salt from the sea that made me think of my lover and my friends across the water. The same questions haunted me; had they given up hope of reaching me? Where was Carl?

Despite these torturing worries I was determined not to give in. It would be better to remain here forever than submit to another of her arranged marriages, and when, every second week, I received a letter from her asking if I was ready to obey, I tore it across and gave the pieces back to the messenger as my reply.

The weeks dragged on. Sometimes, on warm evenings, I climbed to the battlements and watched the sunset. While there was still light I would walk from side to side, looking down at the miles of countryside spread below; much of it belonged to me, yet here I was, a virtual prisoner.

To the east there was a glimpse of the rugged seacoast and a hint of blue water; to the west the moors rolled to the Cheviot hills, spotted here and there with clumps of vivid golden gorse, moors that would soon be one great stretch of purple heather. There was wilder country to the north—dark forests through which the river Aln glinted like a silver ribbon; and, to the south, farms, villages, and towns.

All of it beautiful, all of it remote. Then, as the darkness fell, I would hear the rattling call of the nightjar, shiver with sadness and loneliness, and climb back to my rooms to crawl into bed without even the comfort of my beloved cat.

I asked Lady Lucy, one day, whether my grandmother had ever mentioned the name of the man she wanted me to marry.

"No," she replied. "All she told me was that she had settled on one of the wealthiest men in England and that you would be a fool not to agree."

"The fact that she has not said who it is makes me think there must be something wrong with him—as there was with Henry Ogle."

"I don't know, Lisa, I just don't know. I wish I could do something, but, as always, I'm helpless."

The heather bloomed, dulled, died. The weather turned cool, many days were gray with rain, and the castle grew chillier and draftier. The only break in our dreary existence was the arrival of Grandam's letters, and, by the tenth of October, when another was due, I wondered whether I would have the courage this time to tear it up and face the coming winter.

To our surprise, the messenger brought this one to Lady Lucy, not to me. She read it and handed it to me. "We're to leave immediately and join her at Northumberland House. She has sent an armed escort to bring us there."

I scanned the few lines rapidly, hoping to find some hint of what this meant. Perhaps King Charles had commanded her to bring me back to London! perhaps she had given up the plan to marry me against my will. But I could read no more into it than Lady Lucy, and after discussing the matter for a little while we both decided that I might as well obey. Once safely in town, perhaps I could find someone to speak to the King in my behalf.

I spent much of our uneventful journey holding imaginary defiant scenes with my grandmother or trying to think of ways to reach King Charles, to send word to Princess Mary, to learn somehow, where Carl was now. I even planned several escapes from Northumberland House. . . .

On our arrival Grandam welcomed us with a casualness that astounded both Lady Lucy and me. She did not mention my marriage, which gave me the hope that the man involved had refused to wait any longer for such a reluctant bride, but this, of course, was just a hope. Without saying so, however, she made it clear that I was still a prisoner and I had to depend on Lady Lucy for news of my friends' whereabouts.

It was all disheartening. The King was at Audley End, near Cambridge, and would remain there for several weeks.

Harry Sidney was with him. Lady Temple was out at Sheen with her husband. Lady Mary, the Countess of Dorset, was down at Knole.

While I was wandering restlessly around my apartments, trying to think of what to do next, Lady Lucy came in again looking desperately unhappy.

"I'm being sent down to Petworth," she told me, "to set the house in order for the winter."

"Then I will be truly alone," I said.

I watched my elderly cousin limp out into the great square courtyard and haul herself clumsily up the steps of the traveling coach. After it rolled away I returned to my own apartments, feeling only half alive and stranded on a small island surrounded by fog. There was now no one to talk to but Dolly; my days were empty, my nights disturbed by uneasy dreams.

I ate some of my meals with my grandmother and we sat together occasionally in the evening, but we were strangers, exchanging a few polite remarks for the sake of the servants, a chill smile if we passed each other in one of the long galleries. This, I decided, was her new plan to force me into submission—to freeze me into it.

While the weather was still open enough for a daily walk in the gardens my situation was not too impossible, but when chill, pouring rains kept me indoors I lost my appetite and grew so restless that I often saw Dolly looking at me anxiously, shaking her head at the way my gowns hung on me and commenting on the dark shadows under my eyes.

I was staring listlessly at the calendar on my desk one day, noticing that it was the first of November. The door opened and my grandmother strode in.

"Why were you not at the table last night, Lisa?" she asked me. "Are you ill?"

I shrugged. "I wasn't hungry."

"I must send for some medicine that will give you an appetite. In the meantime, perhaps a change will help. I go to Whitehall today to play cards with the Queen, and I think I'll take you with me. Dress suitably—not your weeds."

My first impulse was to refuse; then I realized that if the Court had moved back to town I might see the King. Even a moment would be enough to ask for his help. So, with high hopes, I told Dolly to fetch my loveliest gown—an apricot satin—and my warmest sable-lined cloak.

A few minutes with her needle made the robe fit a little better, and a final glance in the looking glass was not too discouraging. The shadows and hollows in my face were proof, certainly, that I was miserable and unhappy and needed his Majesty's assistance.

Lady Percy turned to me, when our party reached the Stone Gallery at Whitehall Palace, and indicated some empty chairs at the far end. "Sit there with Lady Haddon and Mistress Bancroft," she said, "and amuse yourselves while I have my game with the Queen."

Her two ladies curtsied their agreement and she hurried off, leaving us to do as she said. The gallery, I soon realized, was emptier than I had expected and I did not see a single familiar face. After my companions were settled and had been deep in conversation for some time, I rose.

"I'm going to one of the retiring rooms," I told them. "Don't disturb yourselves; I know the way, and I won't be gone more than a few minutes."

As I left the Stone Gallery I paused for a moment by one of the guards. "Where is his Majesty today?" I asked him. "Will we see him this afternoon?"

He shook his head. "Not today, my lady. I believe he's on his way to Windsor, and the Queen and her ladies will follow him there tomorrow."

So that was why my grandmother had been willing to bring me here! I was stupid not to have guessed as much.

With a sigh I decided to spend a little while in the retiring room as I had said I would, walking there slowly and remembering vividly the day I had met King Charles and Frisky in this same corridor. The small chamber was empty, but before I had more than stepped inside a simply gowned, pleasant-faced lady followed me and closed the door behind us.

"I beg your pardon," she said rather hesitantly, "but are you not the Lady Ogle?"

Startled, I said I was.

"Ah!" Now she beamed and came to my side. "Then my long search is over at last. My name is Mary Potter and I am a friend of Carl von Königsmark, so listen carefully, for we must not waste a moment in unnecessary talk. Carl has had to return to Sweden, but before he left he asked me to find you somehow and, if you are willing, to arrange a proxy marriage for you with him. Another friend, Colonel Brett, will help us, and once the ceremony is performed we will put you on board a ship for Sweden, where Carl will wed you again in accordance with Swedish law."

My heart gave a great bound. Carl had not forgotten me; all these weeks he had been planning to rescue me! And he obviously did not care any longer about my inheritance.

"But how—when—?" I found myself almost stuttering in my joy and excitement.

"As soon as possible. Leave everything to us, my dear, and come to the water stairs at Northumberland House tomorrow morning. Could you do that?"

"I will," I promised her firmly. "I'll do it somehow!"

"Then be there at ten of the clock in a warm cloak with a hood to hide your hair. Bring nothing with you. I'll see to all that. At the water steps, alone tomorrow at ten. Don't fail us!"

Giving me a comforting pat, she turned back to the door. "I'll join Colonel Brett now and tell him all is well. Until the morning, my dear child."

Our two ladies were still chatting comfortably when I returned to the Stone Gallery, and I sank into my chair with my head spinning. It was almost impossible to sit quietly and wait for my grandmother to finish her game but I forced myself to do so, thanking God that no one was paying any attention to me.

The time passed somehow, and eventually we were all back at Northumberland House. Later that evening Grandam came to my apartments and, without saying anything to me, handed Dolly a small glass vial.

"Give your mistress one teaspoon of this before she retires," she told her curtly, "and two more after her breakfast tomorrow morning."

Turning to me she said, "It's strong and may make you feel odd, but I've been assured it will soon restore your appetite and energy. So I'll expect to see you at the table, ready to eat your dinner."

As anything that would make me stronger and more able

to carry out my part in Carl's plan was more than welcome, there was certainly no need to urge me to try her medicine. After I had swallowed it and gone to bed I *did* feel odd, not stronger, but peaceful and calm. My fears drifted away and although I did think wistfully that I would miss many dear friends when I was living in Sweden—Princess Mary, Lady Temple, even Charles Seymour—I fell asleep quite ready to do anything that would unite me with Carl.

When I awakened I was not so relaxed; indeed, I began to worry about how I was to reach to water stairs without being stopped; where and how a proxy marriage could take place and be binding for someone under age; whether, if the ceremony *was* performed that day, Mistress Potter and her friend would be able to take me to Carl without my grandmother catching us.

Just then Dolly came in with my breakfast, and although I tried to eat I found I was too nervous to do more than swallow a bite or two. By this time I was imagining all sorts of things, even wondering whether I was a fool to trust these strangers. If only, I told myself, there was someone older and wiser than I to tell me what to do!

Soon after I took the larger potion that Dolly had ready for me I began to feel much better. My doubts faded and I went swiftly about the business of making preparations for my escape.

"I want my fur-lined cloak, Dolly," I said. "I'm going to walk in the garden this morning."

Grumbling to herself, for Dolly hated venturing out in the chilly world at this time of year, she fetched it, then went off to don her own warm garments. While she was gone I found a velvet pouch, stuffed into it my pearls, a miniature of my father, and a pair of gloves, hid it under my cloak, and glanced around the room, saying a silent farewell to it and everything in it.

When Dolly returned we descended the stairs and walked to the door that led into the pleasure grounds. The lackey who opened it for us smiled and bowed as we passed, but no one else seemed to notice us at all, and, as I hoped and expected, the paths in the brown and dreary garden were empty.

The moment we were outside I gave an exclamation of disgust. "I've forgotten my gloves, Dolly! Run back for them, please. I'll wait here for you."

As soon as the door closed behind her I was on my way to the river's edge. It was time and the boat should be there. My head was swimming a little as I ran, but I decided it was because I had taken my grandmother's medicine on an almost empty stomach; the fresh air would clear it, I was sure.

To my great relief the water stairs were as empty as the gardens and as I stood on them, shaking my head to clear it, a small craft pulled in quickly. I saw Mistress Potter smiling at me while a rather handsome man with a black mustache like the King's held out a large hand and helped me into the rocking vessel.

"Well done, my dear child!" said my new friend warmly, settling me down on the seat beside her. "This is Colonel Brett, and we have everything arranged for you. You'll be the Countess of Königsmark before noon and, with luck and a favorable wind, well out to sea by this time tomorrow."

I thanked her and gave Colonel Brett a nod and smile. "Where are you taking me now?" I asked them. "I know nothing of proxy marriages."

"To the Fleet," replied Colonel Brett, flashing white teeth at me. "They have their own rules and regulations inside the prison precincts, and anyone can be wed there without banns or special licenses. Even a little maid like you."

The Fleet—but of course. I remembered having heard of it and its runaway marriages. But were they really legal?

Colonel Brett laughed when I raised the question. "Yours will be, certainly. The prison chaplain, the Reverend James Colton himself, is waiting for us in the chapel right now. He'll tie the knot tight for you, never fear!"

To my distress, that strange feeling in my head was getting worse instead of better, and as I stared at a family of swans drifting along near our boat they seemed blurred. After that I was vaguely aware that we had passed the checkerboard gardens of Arundel House, the elaborate Italianate pleasure grounds of Essex House, and the mass of trees and open fields that were part of the Temple.

The shore line changed and we slipped by one vast wooden wharf after another, crowded with ships of all kinds and sizes; now we had turned into Old Fleet Ditch, renamed the New Canal after the Great Fire, and as our boatmen sculled slowly through the narrow waterway the grim walls of Bridewell loomed on my left.

A moment later I saw two St. Pauls on my right, we had passed under Fleet Bridge, and we were pulling over to a busy wharf. Colonel Brett all but lifted me out onto the landing, Mistress Potter was instantly on my other side, and I clung to them both, trying to control my trembling legs.

"I—feel strange," I managed to say in a thick voice very unlike my own. "I'm giddy—"

"Of course you are," said Mistress Potter soothingly. "I would be, too. Come, lean on us—we haven't far to go. There's the visitors' entrance to the prison. Through there and into the chapel—"

I remember very little of what happened after that. The buzzing in my head had increased, and when I found myself facing a man in a black stuff gown with white linen bands who asked me questions I could barely hear them. Someone in a dark velvet coat was standing beside me, his face a blur, his voice far away.

He said, "I, Thomas, take thee, Elizabeth—"

Another voice was telling me to say something. "I, Elizabeth—" words I had said years before, all but forgotten now. Dark clouds gathered in front of my eyes; I was being led back to the door, but this time I didn't know who was supporting me.

When we reached the courtyard the bracing air cleared my senses for a moment, and I was able to see the livery on a lackey holding open a coach door a few feet away.

"No!" I screamed and tried to free myself, pointing to the Percy lion on the side of the coach. "Mistress Potter— quick—"

I was being lifted off my feet, I was inside the familiar coach—

Just before the blackness closed completely over me I dimly heard my grandmother's voice. "That's right. Here beside me. Put her head on this cushion."

12

I opened my eyes, pushed away a hand holding something pungent under my nose, and sat up. The curtains were drawn against the windows of the rocking coach, but there was enough light for me to see that I was alone with my grandmother and the man in the dark velvet coat. He was middle-aged and stout.

"Ah," said my grandmother briskly. "You're feeling better."

"Perhaps another sniff of this?"

"I don't think she needs it, Tom. See, her color has quite returned. Another minute or two and she will be herself again." Giving one of her more unpleasant laughs, she took the silver vinaigrette from his hand and put it in her bag. "We must remember that our Lisa has had a rather exciting morning!"

Then she turned to me.

"Come," she said. "Pull yourself together, child. I want

to wish you joy and present your new husband, Thomas
Thynne, a good friend of mine. You will be grateful, one
of these days, for the little deception that has provided you
with such an agreeable and suitable bridegroom."

I stared at her. When she finished speaking I began to
understand what had happened, and I sank back on the
cushions, covering my face with my hands.

Everything fell into place; it was all dreadfully clear. How
could I have been so gullible, knowing that my grandmother would stoop to anything to achieve her ends? Mistress Potter and Colonel Brett had been working for her,
not Carl. That was why she took me to Whitehall. That
was why she gave me that potion. I was drugged or I would
not have been so stupid! The empty gardens, the whole
scheme was painfully obvious to me now, but oh! how easy
I had made it for her and this toad in the dark coat! When
I raised my head at last our coach was turning into the
courtyard at Northumberland House, and Thomas Thynne
spoke to me for the first time.

"I shall leave you here in Lady Percy's care for a little
while, my lady. Not from any lack of ardor, believe me, but
because I know you will need time to forgive me for win-
ning you in such an unusual fashion. And although I have
had a dozen workmen busy day and night down at Long-
leat making beautiful a suite of rooms for my lovely bride,
they are not yet finished. So, with your permission, I shall
ride there today and return to claim you in a week or so."

He took my icy fingers in his fat, damp hands and raised
them to his lips. Even this light, formal kiss sent shudders
of revulsion through my body, and I jerked my hand away
and hid it under my cloak. There was nothing to say,
nothing.

I was still silent when he helped me out of the coach

and bade me farewell, and I said nothing while my grandmother and I entered the house and walked toward the staircase.

She was silent, too, until we reached the door of my withdrawing room; then she turned to me and dismissed me with a few cold sentences.

"The deed is done, Elizabeth. Scenes and tears will not change anything, so please spare us both. Thomas Thynne is one of the wealthiest gentlemen in England and one of the best born; there's no reason why you should not be content and happy together, so resign yourself to the inevitable and behave as a Percy should."

She took a step down the gallery, then turned back.

"By the way, I must hurry off to Syon House early in the morning, but I'll return to you here long before Tom joins us again."

I found Dolly waiting for me by the fire, and although she said nothing as she helped me out of my cloak, it was clear that she was worried. I'm sure she had reason, for I must have been behaving very strangely. I knew I could neither eat nor drink, and I remember huddling in a chair by the leaping flames all afternoon and evening, staring blindly at nothing.

When a clock struck nine I allowed her to undress me and fell on the bed, turning my face away before she could extinguish the candles. She bade me good night in a tearful voice, and a few minutes later I heard her sobbing softly in her small bed in the corner.

Eventually the sobs stopped and she began to snore, but I lay stiffly on my pillows, dry-eyed and wide awake, my heart pounding in my breast with a suffocating beat. Trapped, it seemed to be saying; trapped, trapped, trapped.

Aching from head to foot and throughly miserable, I rose the next morning at the usual hour. I forced myself to speak to Dolly from time to time, to eat a few bites of bread, to don my clothes. But after that I returned to my chair, still too shocked to think clearly or to ask myself if there was anything I could do to escape from this new web.

Dolly came in, an hour or so later, and stood in front of me, her face so anxious that I tried to smile reassuringly.

"There's a Mistress Trevor insisting on seeing you, my lady," she said. "I told her you were ill, but she said she *must* see you today, immediately, that she has something to tell you that concerns your marriage to Mr. Thynne."

All I could think of was that this was undoubtedly some fresh scheme of my grandmother's to embroil me in more misery; then I remembered that one of the Queen's ladies was a Mistress Trevor. Whatever her reason for coming to me, perhaps she would take pity on me and carry a message to the King.

"Bring her to me here, Dolly," I said, "and see that we have wine and saffron cakes."

I rose, straightened my gown, and patted my hair into place. The door opened and a young woman entered, followed, to my astonishment, by a nursemaid carrying a blanketed infant in her arms.

"Mistress Trevor?" I began, a bit hesitantly, not knowing what to say or how to greet her. All the usual phrases seemed inappropriate somehow.

"So the lawyers tell me," was her reply. Her voice was bitter, her eyes strained, and her face so thin that I could see little of the beauty for which I had heard the Queen's Mistress Trevor praised. "But until a few weeks ago I thought I was Mistress Thomas Thynne. Now they say that our wedding ceremony was a joke, that the man who wed us was one of Tom's cronies, dressed up as a clergyman.

Tom won't answer my letters or see me or his baby! Then I heard that he was planning to marry *you* and I've come to beg you not to, to at least give me time to prove somehow that I am his wife, that I must be his wife—" Her voice broke and she held out her hands to me in a pleading gesture.

I took them and led her to a chair. "Take the infant and its nurse to another room, Dolly," I told my tiring woman. "I'll ring when we want you."

As soon as I was alone with my visitor I sat down beside her. "I'm afraid it is too late," I said. "My grandmother tricked me into marrying Mr. Thynne just yesterday." Then, as she stared at me in horrified silence, I related *my* story. "If you find it hard to believe," I finished, "I will not be surprised. I wouldn't believe such a wild tale."

"I might believe that either of us is telling the truth," she commented, shaking her head, "but hearing that one man could take part in two such deceptions would shock anyone. My ceremony a mock one, with me thinking it a real marriage; yours a legal one, with you thinking it a proxy wedding you to someone else. The whole thing is incredible!" She laughed bitterly. "If it were a play, the audience would boo it off the stage!"

"In any case," I said, "I'm glad you came to me. I've been sitting here feeling helpless and dazed. Now I know that I won't live with that man as his wife no matter what happens! I shall ask for an annulment because Thomas Thynne had a previous contract with you."

"Oh, Lady Ogle, if you would, if you could—"

"I'll try, certainly," I went on, my spirits rising with every word. "My one hope is to see the King and ask him to intervene for us both. But how to reach him is another matter. He's at Windsor, they tell me, and I'm shut up here." I was so accustomed to being a prisoner that it took me a moment to realize that I just might be able to take advantage of Lady Percy's absence if I acted swiftly.

Once the idea occurred to me, I did not waste another moment. I rang for Dolly and said I wanted my cloak and some of my jewels.

"I have no money," I explained to Mistress Trevor. "But if I succeed in walking out of here with you—and I am going to try—I can sell something and hire a boat to take me up the Thames to Windsor."

"I have several pounds with me," said my new friend, "and my coach is waiting in the courtyard."

"Take me to the nearest wharf, then."

"If it weren't for the baby, I'd go with you."

"I will be with my lady," said Dolly firmly. She had brought me the things I wanted and, with them, her own cloak. Her face was set in such stubborn lines that I did not argue; actually, I was grateful for her loyal company.

"Come along, if you insist," I told her. "But you may be sorry. God knows where this will all end, Dolly."

❧

Why no one stopped me from leaving Northumberland House I do not know. Perhaps my grandmother thought me too ill and crushed to rebel in any way; perhaps the servants had not been given the right orders. Happily, my plan succeeded and within the hour Dolly and I were safely on our way to Windsor.

November, of course, is a miserable time to travel by water. The air was chill, and not long after we made our bargain with a boatman and climbed into his small craft a cold rain began to fall. Dolly and I endured the discomfort in silence; then, when we were soaked through, I remembered that Lady Temple was at Sheen. Her home lay on the river somewhere between London and Windsor.

We would break our journey there, I decided instantly. Lady Temple would make us welcome, I knew, and would, when she had heard my story, help me to reach King Charles.

I will not describe in detail the trouble we had finding the Temples' house, nor the argument with the boatman over his fee. Long before we reached our destination I had begun to worry, thinking we might find the house deserted, the Temples in Holland or France.

I was on the verge of tears when Dolly and I finally disembarked at their landing, found the path, and ran through the rain to the handsome, half-timbered building set back some hundred feet from the riverbank; after more time spent knocking on the door, asking a lackey to announce our arrival to his mistress, and waiting for Lady Temple to come to us, I was truly distraught.

Then I heard feet hurrying along a corridor, a dear, familiar figure rushed into the room, and I was in Lady Temple's comforting arms, sobbing wildly on her shoulder.

13

As the Temple coach pulled up the hill to Windsor Castle it was apparent that not only were the King and Queen in residence—their flags were fluttering on the top of the old keep—but that some unusual festivity was in progress.

"I wonder what it can be? I've heard nothing of the Court for some weeks now," said Lady Temple, nodding to a friend in one of the coaches that toiled along beside ours. For the last mile or so the road had been crowded with handsome vehicles all heading our way, and when we turned into the cobbled courtyard of the castle itself we were immediately surrounded by a seething mass of nobles on horseback, more coaches, townspeople dodging around on foot, and what seemed to be an army of servants, pushing shoving and shouting as they tried to make way for their masters and mistresses.

I looked at all this confusion with dismay. How could I possibly hope to have a private audience with King Charles today? But when I said this to Lady Temple she told me not to worry.

"If we can't arrange it today," she said, "we'll stay here until we can. An ancient aunt of William's lives in one of the grace and favor houses, and she'll give us beds for as long as we need them. She's a dear old thing—although she talks all the time! But what *can* be happening here today?"

Once we were out of the coach her question was soon answered. There was to be a great wrestling match in the meadow below the castle terrace. Twelve of the King's men were to be matched against a dozen fighting for the Duke of Albemarle; it would begin within the hour, we were told, and a guard, standing in an arch on that side of the castle, informed Lady Temple that the Queen and many of the ladies were to sit on the terrace and watch the contest from there.

I saw Lady Temple reach into the velvet pouch at her waist and smiled at the ease with which a coin changed hands. A moment later we were whisked through a small doorway on one side of the archway, the guard pointed down a corridor, gave Lady Temple careful instructions for reaching the terrace, bowed, smiled, and ran back to his post.

The sight of several other ladies hurrying ahead of us made Lady Temple laugh. "That guard is having a profitable day," she said. "Well, come along, Lisa. Make haste, my dear. We want seats, too."

I was glad to obey. Still weary from the physical and emotional stresses of the last two days, I had no desire to stand for the rest of the morning. For another thing, my borrowed shoes were a little tight; my own were still soaked, the wherry having shipped a great deal of water as we tacked our way to Sheen, and Lady Temple had provided me with a pair that had belonged to her daughter Diana.

While I was trying them on, my hostess had slipped away, returning with a beautiful gray-green velvet gown over her arm. "This was Diana's favorite robe," she had told me, her eyes misty. "Her hair was fair, of course, but it should look very well on you, my dear, with your flaming head."

My protest had gone almost unheard. "I want you to wear it," she had insisted, handing it to Dolly.

Now, as we pushed through the jostling, laughing, chattering crowd of richly garbed ladies, I was glad to be wearing it; I would have felt conspicuous indeed in my simple morning gown and hooded traveling cloak. But this charming velvet costume, with its gleaming satin underdress and delicious deep green bows, was as pretty as anything I saw around me. And the great square sable muff and warm, soft matching tippet (Lady Temple had called it by the new French name "pelerine"), which belonged to Lady Temple herself, were so lovely that I wondered how she could bear to lend them to me.

Another coin or two from the pouch and a short scurry after a royal liveried lackey calling out, "Way, make way for the Countess of Ogle! Way, way for Lady Temple!" took us through a roped-off part of the terrace and into a pair of empty chairs. In the center, under a gilded satin draped canopy, was Queen Catherine's chair of state.

Just as we were settling into our seats the sound of trumpets brought us back to our feet, and the shrill voice of her Majesty's usher sent us down in deep court curtsies.

This was my first glimpse of the royal lady and I was glad when Catherine of Braganza waved us all into our chairs, for only then was I able to see her face. I knew she had never been a beauty, but the passing of time had apparently been unkind to the dark-eyed, dark-haired, olive-skinned Portuguese.

"She's so fat and dumpy!" I said to Lady Temple. "She doesn't look a bit like a queen."

"She never did," replied my companion. "When she came to England to marry Charles she was tiny and graceful—quite charming, really, in a gypsylike way. But she's not been too happy, you know, and so she overeats."

I settled back and studied the scene below us. A ring had been formed in the meadow to encircle the competitors, and King Charles's gilded painted coach stood inside it so he could watch in cosy comfort.

Just then Lady Temple pointed to a tall man in vivid blue, moving around in the crowd below the terrace. Before she spoke my heart jumped, for I thought at first glance that it was Carl. Needless to say, I had been thinking of him constantly, wondering if he might be at Court or if anyone here would know of his whereabouts. What he could do, or say, about my ghastly situation I had no idea; but I longed to throw myself into his arms and tell him myself just how my grandmother had used his name to achieve her ends.

"That's Chris Monck," said Lady Temple, "the Duke of Albemarle." As she indicated him, I saw that it was not Carl. "And here come the wrestlers. The ones in blue waist-coats will be Chris's men, those in red his Majesty's."

I counted them and sighed. It would take all day!

But it was surprising how swiftly one match followed another, and long before I thought it possible the twelfth wrestler was pinned to the ground and the King emerged from his coach to award the prize money to the blues. Assuming this was the end of the day's sport, I prepared to rise. To my distress, they all came back in the ring and fought each other with swords, following that with a rough game of football. When I realized that the King's men had lost every match, my spirits fell even lower. "He'll be in a black mood," I said to Lady Temple. "He won't want to see anyone."

"Nonsense." She laughed. "He's the best sportsman in England! Win or lose, he enjoys every minute of these contests."

It seemed she was right, for he emerged from his coach and shouted out an enthusiastic speech of thanks for the day's sport. At the end of it he went inside again, and the gaudy vehicle began to move slowly up the slope to the castle.

This was the signal for everyone to disperse, and as we trailed after the Queen and her ladies, who were leading the way inside the great building, a group of gentlemen from the meadow caught up with us and I saw that one of them was my cousin Harry.

Before I could tell Lady Temple, he was beside us, greeting us both warmly. "Dorothy!" he said delightedly. "And my little Lisa! Where have you been all these months, my child? And how do you happen to be here without your grandmother?"

"Find us a quiet corner, Harry," replied Lady Temple, "and we will tell you all about it. Lisa must have a private audience with King Charles at the first possible moment, and you are just the man to arrange it for us."

❧

A half hour later Lady Temple and I were sitting in the gallery, watching the curtain that hung over the entrance to the King's audience chamber. Harry Sidney was in there, we knew, appealing to his Majesty on my behalf. "He has spoken of you more than once," Harry told us after I had finished my incredible story. "Just recently he said he was growing tired of Lady Percy's evasions and excuses."

While we waited, Lady Temple tried to set me more at ease by pointing out the beauties of the royal apartments. "King Charles has introduced fresh elegance at Windsor," she said. "Verrio painted these wonderful ceilings, and someone named Grinling Gibbons carved those enchanting garlands of fruit and flowers. Some say he's an Englishman, some that he's from Holland. I think—"

I was not to know what she thought, for Harry reappeared at that moment and hurried to where we were sitting.

"Madam Gwyn is with him now," he whispered, "but he has promised to send for you, Lisa, as soon as her audience is over. I'm glad it's Nelly. She always leaves him in a merry humor."

I had heard so many amusing tales of the poor orange girl who first became England's most popular actress, then left the stage to live in luxury as one of King Charles's mistresses, that I hoped for a glimpse of her. Sure enough, a few minutes later I saw a dainty little woman with a dimpled, laughing face slip through the curtain and walk down the long gallery, exchanging gay bits of banter with many of the lords and ladies as she passed by. I was so interested that, when my name was suddenly called aloud, I almost jumped out of my seat.

"The Countess of Ogle, if you please. His Majesty will see Lady Ogle."

Rising to my feet, my legs trembling under me, I turned, gave my friends a wobbly smile, and walked up the miles of gallery lined with curious, glittering, staring eyes. My hands were icy cold and I was almost faint with fright as I followed the usher into the inner room and dipped down in my deepest curtsy, vaguely aware that there was no one in the audience chamber but the tall man on the great carved throne.

"Come here, my dear child, and sit on this stool near me." The royal voice was so warmly welcoming that my courage rose and I moved more swiftly across the room to the little cushioned seat in front of the dais.

"First let me tell you," he said, as I kissed his long fingers, "how charming you look in that gown. I'm glad our Countess Carrots has discarded her dreary weeds!"

I told him how Princess Mary had effected the change, and before I knew it the King and I were chatting easily about her Highness's health and life at The Hague. He guided me skillfully from one topic to another, drawing from me the whole shocking story of my marriage to Thomas Thynne and everything I knew about his betrayal of Mistress Trevor.

"If this were not the seventeenth century," he commented finally, his gaunt face set in deep, stony lines and his eyes angry, "I would throw Thynne and your grandmother into the Tower. As I cannot, I must send you to safety until our lawyers find a way to annul that infamous ceremony."

Before he could say anything more, I blurted out my love for Carl and the details of his unsuccessful courtship.

"Help us, your Majesty," I pleaded. "Free me from that dreadful Mr. Thynne and let me marry Carl!"

He looked down at me and sighed. "I presented the handsome rascal to you myself, did I not? I can only say I'm sorry; he's not the husband I'd choose for you, my dear. But we shall not look that far into the future yet; first we must see what the law says. And in the meantime, I think I'll send you back to Princess Mary."

When the King of England takes you under his wing, everything moves swiftly. Two days later, on November seventh to be exact, I stood with Harry Sidney on the deck of the royal yacht, watching for the small boat that would take him back on shore. Lady Temple, who was accompanying me to The Hague, was below, settling our few belongings before we raised anchor and set sail.

This was the first moment I'd had alone with my cousin, and, as it could well be the last, I asked him the question that had been on my lips since our encounter at Windsor.

"Tell me, Harry," I said, "have you seen or heard anything of Carl Königsmark recently?"

He looked at me in silence, hesitated, then replied. "Yes, Lisa, I have. He's been in London several times in the last few months—trying to find you, I gather, and visiting his young brother Philip, who's a student at Foubert's Academy. As a matter of fact, I ran into him myself at Whitehall one evening, and he told me he'd heard from someone you were at Alnwick, but when he rode up there he wasn't allowed inside the walls."

"Oh!" I gave a great sigh of relief. He hadn't forgotten me. I reached in my bag and took out a letter. "Would you see that he receives this? I can't let him hear of my marriage and not tell him how it happened. You can understand that, can't you?"

"Well," he said slowly, "I suppose I can. But look here, Lisa, if I do this errand for you—and I probably shouldn't —you must promise me that there will be no more masquerades, no secret meetings, no elopements. This is no time to have a lover sighing after you, you know; you're in enough trouble as it is."

I nodded. "I do know, Harry. Lady Temple said the same thing when she agreed to come with me—that any gossip about me at this particular time might influence the court in giving me an annulment, and that it would be another weapon in Grandam's hands. I do see that you are both right, and I do promise you, gladly."

He smiled at me, tucked my letter into his large pocket, and pointed to a small boat nearing the side of the yacht. "Here I go, my dear. Tell our friends at The Hague that I hope to be there for Christmas."

As he kissed me farewell, Lady Temple joined us, and after we watched him climb down the swaying ladder and take his seat in the rocking vessel we stayed at the rail, waving, until it was nothing but a tiny bobbing shape, leaving a lacy trail on the water.

Our own vessel suddenly came alive. Orders were shouted from the captain's bridge over our heads, feet pattered on the decks, ropes creaked, canvas flapped, and then we heard the soft sibilance of the ship cutting through the deepening river.

The Thames widens at Gravesend, and fresher breezes from the sea made us draw our cloaks more closely around us. But although I realized that I might be leaving Carl behind me, the salty smell was, at this moment, the perfume of freedom, leading to a faint hope of happier days ahead.

14

Princess Mary met me with outstretched arms and such a warm and welcoming face that tears filled my eyes. The November seas had been rough, our voyage long and miserably uncomfortable, and when we landed at last and finally reached The Hague it was not the charming, sunny, delightful city I remembered. The tall houses seemed to brood darkly over the streets, the leafless trees were a grim reminder of cold months to come, and the ancient buildings around the gray lake looked as if they might house ogres.

I returned Mary's embrace with fervor, more grateful than I could say to find her even happier to see me than I had expected. Here, within the old palace, was something that lifted my heart as the brightest sunshine could not, something better than the bluest of skies.

I think we both started to talk at once; then, after she had greeted Lady Temple and we were all seated, I gave her a letter from King Charles.

She read it carefully. "My uncle says you come to me, Lisa, at his suggestion. He requests me to keep you with me until he has settled several questions concerning your future. But he doesn't tell me what those questions are. Is he arranging your marriage to Carl?" The moment she finished speaking she put her hand over her mouth and looked at Lady Temple with such guilty eyes that I almost laughed.

"It's all right," I assured her. "Lady Temple knows all my secrets now. No, he's trying to help me in another way."

As we three were alone, I immediately told her everything that had happened to me since our parting that summer. When I finished the long tale she gazed at me with incredulous horror.

"I think my uncle Charles *should* have thrown Lady Percy into the Tower!" she exclaimed. "It's inhuman—it's criminal—it's—"

"He sent me to you," I said. "And he promises to do what he can to annul my marriage. I couldn't ask more than that."

❧

Later, when Lady Temple had set out for home again, I had another private talk with the Princess. This time we both spoke more freely, and I unburdened my heart. "You are the only one who understands how I feel about Carl," I told her. "The King, Cousin Harry, Lady Temple—they all disapprove, for some reason, and I've had to promise not to meet him secretly or do anything that could cause gossip while I am here with you."

"They're all too old to remember what it means to be deeply in love," was her reply. "And I suppose they think about your fortune, Lisa. If you marry a foreigner much of it might go out of England—I don't know, but that could be a reason."

She sighed and gave me a wistful smile. "In the meantime, let's try to forget our troubles for a while and enjoy ourselves, if we can. I—" Her voice broke, and I saw the ready tears fill her eyes and sparkle on the tips of her dark lashes. "I've been desperately unhappy, too."

For the first time I noticed that her face was thinner and that she looked very unwell. "I'm a selfish beast," I said, remorsefully, taking her small hand in mine. "I've talked of nothing but myself from the moment I arrived! What is wrong, your Highness? Tell me."

"Something that's been wrong for years, and I've only recently learned about it. From my own father, in a letter. It—it's a shaming thing, Lisa, to hear that your husband and one of your childhood friends have been carrying on an intrigue under your very eyes for years and years! My father writes that it began before William and I were married and has been going on ever since. Everybody knows it, apparently. I suppose you do, too."

I felt the color flooding my cheeks, and I dropped my eyes. "I—well, there's always gossip around a royal household."

"But is it just gossip? I keep telling myself that it is and that my father can have no proof. I've hardly slept since his letter arrived, but I can't ask William—I can't! And it's torture having Betty Villiers near me now, but I must be sure before I dismiss her. You can see that, Lisa?"

Indeed I could. I could also see that knowing the truth might make her unhappier than ever, but I didn't say so.

"Then why don't we do what you just suggested, your Highness? Enjoy ourselves while we can?"

That evening, after I had changed into the green velvet gown and taken my place in the dismal hall with the rest of the royal guests, I found myself staring at Betty Villiers and wondering how and why she had caught William's fancy and held it for so long. She was redheaded—of course, I can never see beauty in red hair—and had the heavy-lidded protruding Howard eyes that always remind me painfully of my grandmother; her mouth, in repose, was like Lady Percy's too, supercilious and cruel. In fact, the only thing about my kinswoman that I could honestly admire was a pair of unusually neat little ears, set close to her head.

I was still pondering the matter as I made my curtsy to William and Mary. The royal couple, walking slowly together down the long aisle between the rows of bowing ladies and gentlemen, were silent until they reached their seat on the canopied dais. In his customary stiff manner, the Prince then spoke a few words of general greeting and told his usher to bring up the guests who had not yet been presented.

The rest of us broke up into little chattering groups, and I, caught in the center of one speaking only Dutch, was relieved and pleased when a familiar English voice called me by name.

It was Charles Seymour, the Duke of Somerset, and as I had heard from Mary that he had not been in The Hague for many months, I was surprised as well as delighted to see him.

"Your Grace!" I gave him my hand and a warm smile.

He kissed it, after making such an elegant, graceful leg that I told myself the Grand Tour was turning this shy, quiet young man into a polished gallant. Then I saw a new, provocative glint in his eyes; instead of dropping my fingers, he held them closely in his for longer than was usual and drew me off into a secluded corner.

"Come and tell me why you disappeared so suddenly and mysteriously last summer," he said. "All her Highness would say was that you were summoned home and had no time for farewells. We missed you sadly."

"It's just the way my grandmother does things." I tried to explain. "Go here, go there, come home immediately. I sometimes think she would make a fine army general."

"Is Lady Lucy Hay with you?"

"No, Lady Temple brought me here. I'm staying in the palace as her Highness's guest." For the first time, I realized that it must seem strange for me to be in Holland without the protection of a companion or duenna, and the puzzled expression on Charles's face indicated that he thought so, too.

To my great relief he did not question me further; instead, he talked of the pleasant evenings we had shared at the House in the Woods. "There must be some salon in this gloomy pile where we can dance and play games," he said. "Let's urge her Highness to repeat those happy times we all had together."

❧

As it turned out, neither of us had to urge Princess Mary. She had already decided, she told me the next day, to begin dancing again. "It will cheer us both up," she said, "and I find I don't feel much like cards right now."

She was quite right; it did cheer us up. For several evenings after that she invited both the nobles who lived at The Hague and the foreign visitors, chose a large salon in a secluded wing of the palace, ordered in her musicians, and we all danced to our hearts' content.

Our company grew larger every night, and I heard it whispered that Betty Villiers's supper parties for Prince William's friends were suffering as a result. I did not, of course, mention this to Mary—I don't believe she knew about those parties, although how Betty explained her lack of attendance on Mary had me bewildered.

A week passed, then another, and I began feeling almost young and happy again. All the terrible things that had happened to me in England seemed like a bad dream, an impossible, unbelievable nightmare that could not be true. But although I could forget my troubles for hours at a time, they returned to plague me whenever letters arrived at The Hague from King Charles. It was too soon to expect word of my annulment, but I could not help hoping, praying—

Then something else began to worry me. It struck me as ridiculous the first time Mary teased me about it, but after a while I had to admit that she could be right. Charles Seymour came to every one of our dancing evenings, with never a thought, apparently, of continuing his travels or returning home. Mary insisted that he was falling in love with me and was remaining in The Hague to court me, and when his attentions became more and more marked I grew quite concerned.

He was much too nice to hurt, but although I knew I should not allow him to lose his heart, I had no idea how to prevent it. I was reluctant to tell him of either my love for Carl or my marriage to Thomas Thynne; after much thought, I decided to adopt a colder, more impersonal manner with him and perhaps to stay away from some of Mary's festivities.

A slight headache gave me a good excuse to remain in my chamber the evening after I came to this decision, but it was not bad enough to make me glad to be there. I tried to read; then, as faint sounds of music reached me, I threw the book down and took up my needlework.

An hour dragged away; I was about to give up and go to bed when a lackey scratched on the door.

"Her Highness would like the Countess Ogle to come to her privy chamber," he told Dolly. "As soon as possible, please."

Wondering what could take Mary away from her guests, and why she wanted me in such a hurry, I tidied my hair and followed the lackey through the dim corridors. He left me just outside the entrance to Mary's withdrawing room and I ran in, curious and a little fearful.

At first I thought the room was empty; then I heard the door close behind me and I was in Carl's arms.

How long I remained there I do not know. When we drew apart, at last, he took me to a wide cushioned seat and sat down beside me. I suppose I expected words of comfort and love; instead, I was subjected to a torrent of questioning that turned my hands and feet to ice and made me feel actually ill.

"How could you have been so stupid, Lisa?" he began, angrily. "If I had arranged a proxy wedding I would have sent you a letter, not just a message by a stranger! I couldn't believe it, when your letter reached me; a child would not be so easily duped! Matters were difficult enough before, but *now*—"

He paused and I tried to explain, but everything I said sounded foolish and unconvincing even to myself. I faltered, swallowed a sob, and buried my face in my shaking hands.

Taking me back in his arms, he kissed me fiercely once or twice, pushed me aside almost roughly, and when he spoke again, his voice was still full of anger.

"You may be sure of this, Lisa—Thynne will never have you. But I will not be patient any longer while the so-clever Lady Percy baits a new trap for you. For the moment you are free to do what you wish. The Princess Mary is our friend and will help us."

I looked at him in bewilderment. What was he talking about? How could I be free to do what I wanted until my marriage had been annulled?

"There's nothing I *can* do, Carl, in my present situation. You must see that."

"I see only that I will not risk losing you now. You must come to me, *mitt hjärta*; we will go to Sweden together. If the courts do not free you I shall then seek out Thynne and force him to meet me on the field of honor, where I promise you I can make you a widow."

"But, Carl." I began protesting, not knowing just what to say. "What you are suggesting frightens me! I—how can I go with you?"

"How can you *not* go with me? You must and you will. I shall think for us both from now on, my sweet, so meet me here tomorrow evening at this same time, and I will tell you then how and when we will leave the palace together."

I returned to my chamber to spend the night in an agony of indecision. The more I thought about Carl's suggestion, the more frightened I became. The idea of running away with him, once my dearest dream, no longer seemed the answer to our problem. Before, I assumed that we would wed and hope my grandmother could not prove the ceremony illegal. Now, we could only elope and live together as lovers, with any marriage a vague possibility in the dim future. This, I told myself, was preferable to a life as Thomas Thynne's wife, but if King Charles did not succeed in annulling that Fleet wedding, what would happen then? I could not take seriously Carl's threat to kill Mr. Thynne.

And although I tried to push them aside, all those stories of Carl's romantic adventures began to creep into my mind: the wellborn ladies in France and Spain, that English girl of good family and erstwhile spotless reputation hiding in a convent with Carl's illegitimate child.

What about a child of my own, nameless, and with a dishonored mother? Suppose I died? Could I expose a child to such an uncertain life? Could I face it for myself?

I tossed from side to side, my pillows hot and rumpled. Finally I listened to a small inner voice asking the worst question of all: What would I do if we could never marry and Carl tired of me?

I rose the next morning weary but with my mind made up. Fortunately, the day was crammed with visitors and activities and I did not have a moment in which to change it, nor did I have an opportunity to confide in Princess Mary. I knew she was eager to hear what had come of my meeting with Carl, but I was spared the need to tell her.

When the time came to join him again that evening, I went to her Highness's privy chamber unhappy but determined. I think he knew my answer as soon as I crossed the threshold; in any event, he listened quietly while I described my sleepless night and the doubts and fears that had assailed me.

"I would spend the rest of my life making you happy," he replied. "It would be a sacred trust."

"But we might have a child," I said again. "No, Carl, I cannot do it. If my marriage is annulled and we can be married according to the laws of Sweden, I will go with you with all my heart. Until then we must wait and I must keep my promise not to meet you in secret again."

There was a long minute of grim silence. Carl's voice, when he spoke at last, was cold, his eyes bleak.

"Very well," he said. "You leave me nothing to say or do. If my love means that little to you, I think I will join an expedition that is sailing soon to relieve Tangiers. With luck, the Moors will kill me this time and our problem will be settled once and for all!"

15

When Carl strode out of Mary's privy chamber without a word of farewell or a backward glance, I returned to my own quarters with my mind in a turmoil. His threat to go and fight the Moors sounded like bravado—from someone else I would assume it was—but from Carl I could not be sure. It was the kind of adventure he had sought before and might well again.

After another restless night I joined Mary and her ladies, and later in the day we did have an hour alone in which I told her what had happened between Carl and me. At first she thought I should have run off with him; then, after I haltingly described my reasons for refusing, she agreed, a little reluctantly, that I made the right decision.

It seemed wise not to take part in the dancing for a few evenings, so I pleaded illness and remained in my chamber. Carl did not appear, Mary told me, and Charles Seymour, after many solicitous inquiries about my health, left The Hague to spend Christmas with friends in Paris.

"Tell Lady Ogle," was his message to me, "that I will return to celebrate the New Year here and look forward to seeing her then."

A day or so later we learned that Carl had indeed set out for Tangiers, and this fresh cause for anxiety, added to my long wait for news of my annulment, made it impossible to enjoy anything. Actually, Christmas was always a quiet family holiday in Holland, and even the New Year would be celebrated, Mary told me, without much in the way of festivities. I did join her and the others every evening, dancing, playing cards, or whatever was planned for our amusement. But I did not enjoy it.

The arrival of my cousin Harry broke the monotony for me, although he could tell me little about my particular business. "The King is still waiting for the Court's decision on your marriage. I don't know why the law is always so slow!"

My grandmother, he said, was spending most of her time at Petworth. Thomas Thynne was roistering about town with the young Duke of Monmouth, King Charles's oldest son; the Temples had moved to their house on Pall Mall for the winter; the Dorsets were in London, too, and had asked him about me more than once.

"I told Lady Mary you were here visiting her Highness. I agree with the King that your story should not be spread around at this point in the proceedings. When the matter is settled, Lisa, and you return to England, you can tell Lady Mary all about it if you wish."

❧

Shortly before New Year's we heard that Charles Seymour and his tutor were back in The Hague, and on New Year's Eve he appeared at the palace. Our company was thin that evening; Prince William had dined with us earlier in the day but did not join his wife at supper, and his absence lowered Mary's spirits so noticeably that we all tried to think of some way to cheer her up.

It was Charles Seymour, finally, who made the best suggestion. "The weather is so unusual for this time of year," he said, "that we should not waste it. It's clear, warm, and the full moon is just beginning to rise. Instead of welcoming in the New Year here, why not call for coaches and ride over for a glimpse of the sea?"

When Mary looked doubtful, he insisted that there was nothing impractical in his plan. The tiny sea village of Scheveningen was less than three miles away, and a tree-bordered avenue ran directly to it from the pleasure grounds behind the palace.

"Well," she said, seeing that most of us were eager to go, "if we can persuade the Princess of Oost Friesland to come with us, I suppose there could be no objection."

She was thinking of Prince William, of course. Without someone to play propriety he might consider such an expedition a frivolous, unseemly frolic.

A word with the good-natured Dutch princess was all that was necessary, and in a very short time we ladies were seated in three large coaches and a party of gentlemen were waiting, mounted on their horses. Whips cracked, coachmen shouted, wheels creaked, hooves clattered, and we were off.

The long straight road stretched out ahead of us, startlingly white in the moonlight, and the leafless trees marched along beside it, looking like ghostly skeletons with their arms pointing up to the night sky.

Sitting beside Anne Trelawney, I shivered inside my fur-lined cloak. I wasn't cold, but there was something so eerie about the stark landscape whirling past the coach windows that I felt as if icy fingers were touching my heart. What was I doing here in this strange flat country? A wave of homesickness swept over me, and I longed for England's hills and valleys, unpredictable lanes and meandering streams. Everything in Holland was so—level, so *straight!*

But when we reached the picturesque village of Scheveningen my fit of the dismals disappeared, for the scene in front of us was pure enchantment. As the coaches pulled up a few yards from the dunes that kept the sea at bay, all the younger members of our party swarmed from the cumbersome vehicles and dismounted from their horses to stand, for a moment, in silent admiration.

Patches of heavy dune grass, still vividly green, climbed here and there on the sandy hillocks; a gap in the taller dunes gave us a glimpse of the ocean, its waves sparkling in the moonlight and breaking in creamy scallops on the beach. The small red-roofed seaside houses lay on our right, their windows dark. A light in the church, where I suppose the bellringers were waiting to ring out the old year and ring in the new, was the only sign of life. Fishermen need their sleep, whatever the date.

The round face of the Princess of Oost Friesland appeared at the coach window. "If you plan to walk to the water's edge, my children, as I suspect you do, go now. I'll sit here and wait for you. But ten minutes, mind, and no more!"

"I'll keep them in order," promised Harry Sidney. "Ten minutes it shall be."

The coachmen drove the coaches a little off the road, and our party started toward the water. Princess Mary took Harry's arm and, laughing and scrambling through the soft sand, they led the way.

After his first cordial greeting earlier that evening Charles Seymour had paid no particular attention to me, but now, when the others climbed around one side of the large dune blocking our path to the sea, he was suddenly at my side, moving me firmly and deftly in the other direction. Before I quite realized what he was doing, or could protest, we were in a deep, shadowed hollow, lined with dune grass and facing right out to the ocean.

The magnificence of the limitless moonlit panorama spread in front of my dazzled eyes made me gasp. I stood there, awed, caught by the magic. From the village, on the other side of the dunes, came the sound of church bells, ringing a somber peal.

"The end of 1681," said Charles softly. "Let it go! I have great hopes for 1682. They say," he murmured, "that you will do all year what you are doing when the new year is born." And as the bells changed their tune he took me swiftly in his arms, his lips seeking mine. I must have been bemused by the moonlight, the soft air, and the unearthly beauty all around us, for when his mouth touched mine I felt my senses quicken.

The bells pealed out triumphantly; my heart beat faster and faster. Charles drew me closer, and for an unthinking, reckless moment my kisses answered his.

"No!" Shocked by my response, I pulled myself free and ran back to the road. I could hear Charles floundering after me but guilt must have put wings on my heels because he was still some distance away when I climbed into the waiting coach. To my great relief I heard the voices and footsteps of the others, approaching from the other direction.

"You missed a beautiful sight, Lisa," said Anne Trelawney. "What happened? One minute you were with us, then you disappeared."

"I turned my ankle in the sand," I lied swiftly. "It was painful for a few moments but it seems quite all right now."

The coach ahead of us moved off; before ours could

follow it Princess Mary and my cousin Harry came to our side and he helped her in.

"William's aunt is snoozing," Mary explained, "so I thought I'd ride with you."

We made room, Harry closed the door, our coach lurched a few feet, then stopped. I heard the pounding of heavy hooves and, looking back, I saw a dark shape coming toward us on the hitherto deserted road. I was still watching when the approaching vehicle drew abreast and passed on. The strange coach had two occupants, sitting close together on the wide seat, both clearly visible in the moonlight.

Recognizing instantly Prince William's square head and Betty Villiers's bright red hair, I reached over to draw the leather curtain across our coach window. A smothered, angry gasp from Mary, followed by a feverish burst of conversation, was proof enough that I had been too late, and although none of us mentioned the incident I think it shook us all.

I, of course, was thoroughly shaken already by my own shameful behavior, and I must confess that my concern over it almost put Mary's unhappy experience out of my mind. I know that I tried, as I disrobed for bed, to ease my conscience by blaming Charles. How dared he spirit me away from our friends and make love to me in such a fashion? How could I guess that anyone as gentlemanly and considerate would suddenly take advantage of my unprotected situation?

But even as I asked myself these questions I knew that I could not this easily shut my eyes to my own guilt. Charles did not force me to go off with him, and I could certainly have avoided his kisses. No, it was my response to his lovemaking that was reprehensible. What kind of wanton was I—in love with Carl, yet hot for another man's caresses?

Morning found me more cheerful, and I ate my bread and cheese with a good appetite, resolving never to allow such a thing to happen again. I would call it a fit of moonlight madness, accept Charles's humble apologies when he made them, and forget the whole incident.

It was the custom in Holland for gentlemen to spend most of New Year's Day calling on the ladies of their acquaintance, and although I did not expect to be very busy myself, I had sufficient callers to pass the time agreeably. Several of our dancing partners from the Embassy dropped in. The young Prince of Oost Friesland arrived with a bowl of tulips so dark they were almost black and remained long enough to tell of the tulip madness that swept over Holland a few years previously. Fortunes had changed hands for single bulbs of rare blossoms, he said, and black tulips were the rarest.

Charles came in on the Prince's heels, completely at his ease and with a charming bouquet of flowers in his hand. As I thanked him for it I saw a note tucked in among the blossoms—his apology, I decided, and kept both my face and my conversation coolly impersonal until he finally said farewell.

I took the folded bit of paper into my bedchamber and read it. It was short and not at all what I expected.

Forgive me if I frightened you last night. But I shan't say I'm sorry. I'm not.

I read it again, telling myself that Charles was not the shy, gentle young man I had thought him. I must actually avoid him from now on—be rude, if necessary.

I was still thinking about this when I joined the others at the supper table. Charles was not among our company, I was glad to see, but Princess Mary was in her place on the dais, looking white and drawn. Prince William was beside her, saying little, as usual; he rose at the end of the meal, announced that as he would be working late that evening he would say good night to all of us now, kissed his wife's hand formally, and left the hall.

We played a few hands of basset afterward, trying to raise Mary's spirits, but the game dragged miserably. I saw her glance repeatedly at the clock and finally, at the end of a dull hand, she threw her cards on the table and said she thought she would retire. "I'm weary tonight. It's been a long day."

I was glad to have it end, too, and I went to my own apartments yearning for my bed. But when I entered my little withdrawing room I found Harry Sidney waiting there for me, holding several letters in his hand.

"I sent your chamberwoman into the other room," he told me. "I have news for you at last, Lisa, and I must see you alone to tell you about it. I think we can forget about propriety for a few minutes."

I nodded, unable to speak. I knew from his face that his news was bad.

"Here is a letter from King Charles." He handed it to me. "I'm sorry, my dear child, but he writes that your marriage to Thynne has been declared legal and he holds out little hope now of an annulment."

"And the—the precontract with Mistress Trevor?"

He shook his head. "No proof. Thynne denies it flatly and refuses to admit any responsibility toward her and the child."

"Then what am I to do, Harry?" A sob rose in my throat, making it difficult to continue. "I won't live with that man—I won't, Harry! I'd rather die!"

"I know, I know. It's a dreadful business—and the worst of it is that he's suing for restitution."

"Restitution?" The word meant nothing to me.

"Marital restitution. He's asking the courts to order you to return to him. However, his suit will take time, thank God, and, in the meantime"—he waved the other paper he was holding—"I have here indications that Thynne bribed Brett and the Potter woman to trick you into the wedding ceremony. We'll see that they are called and cross-examined, and this might well influence the court to refuse his plea."

I drew in a deep, sobbing breath.

"I'm sorry, my dear, sorrier than I can say. Remain here with the Princess, be brave, and avoid even the appearance of any romantic entanglement. It's more important than ever for you to be an innocent maid trapped by a scheming grandmother and a notorious rake. It's lucky that dashing Swede went off to fight the Moors."

I thought of Carl's proposal and said nothing.

"By the way." Harry laughed, and the old amused twinkle returned to his eyes. "You have another suitor. The young Duke of Somerset called on me today and asked me to speak to Lady Percy on his behalf. He's a fine lad, very much in love with you, no fortune hunter, and even your high and mighty grandmother could not call him unsuitable. Unfortunately, all I was able to do was try to spare his feelings; I said I thought he was too late, that Lady Percy was arranging another match for you."

"Should I tell him about Carl?"

"Good God, no! You should not discuss *anything* with him, Lisa. I've warned him off; that's the end of it."

Rising, he walked over to the table where the servants had left refreshments. "It's been a long, hard day. With your permission, I'll have a glass of Hollands and say good night."

He emptied his goblet quickly and I walked with him to

the door, watching him disappear down the dim corridor. An odd rustling noise on the staircase nearby that led up to some bedrooms over mine caught my attention; I listened a moment, then climbed a step or two to see what it was.

There, huddled in a shadowy corner of the landing, was Mary, her face half hidden in a scarf.

"Sh—sh!" Before I could speak she gestured me back, her finger on her lips. "If you love me, Lisa," she whispered, "go away and forget you saw me. Please, before it's too late!"

Too late for what? While I scuttled down again I wondered what in the world she could be doing there and if there was any way in which I could help her. She had sounded so desperate that I did not want to go to bed and leave her there, so I left my door open a crack and waited just inside.

Fifteen long minutes ticked away on my clock, then half an hour. By peering around the door I could just see a bit of Mary's shadow on the staircase wall. I was very tired now, tired enough to tell myself this strange business was none of mine and retire to my bedchamber, when a familiar heavy step sounded down the corridor.

I drew back hastily, remembering for the first time that Betty Villiers slept in one of the rooms over my apartments. And remembering, too, that most of the other chambers on that floor were unoccupied.

Not daring to move or even close the door I stood frozen, my back against the wall. Voices rang out on the staircase, angry voices—Mary's and then Prince William's—followed by a violent burst of weeping and the tread of feet descending the stairs.

"Most husbands would beat their wives for such behavior," I heard William say in a cold, furious voice. "Spying on me like a common kitchen wench! A man's amusement is not a crime, you know, and tonight you've shamed us both past forgiveness."

Sick at heart, I held my breath until they were safely past my door. I closed it then as quietly as possible; without meaning to, I also had spied on William. Had he seen the light from my withdrawing room and noticed that the door was ajar?

16

I was not surprised the next morning to hear that Princess Mary wanted me to come to her bedchamber at my earliest convenience; my thoughts, as I passed reluctantly through the gloomy galleries and antechambers that led to the royal apartments, were not happy. I was sorry for her, naturally, but I was also concerned for myself. Had the Prince glimpsed me hiding inside my door? Was Mary going to tell me I must leave the palace? In my wretched situation, more desperate than ever, where else could I turn for protection?

The appearance of her presence chamber did nothing to allay my forebodings. Accustomed as I was to finding it full of ladies-in-waiting at this time of day, busy with their sewing or reading, buzzing around their royal mistress like bees in a hive, it was disturbing to find it completely empty and in an unusual state of disorder. Was Mary ill and everyone at her bedside?

But when I reached her bedchamber I saw at a glance

that although my dear friend *was* in bed, and propped high on a pile of silken pillows, there was no sign of Anne Trelawney, Mistress Langford, Jane Zulestein, or any of the Villiers sisters. A pair of Dutch chamberwomen were occupied with the royal wardrobe, and another two were standing silently near the great white and gold porcelain stove; except for them the Princess was alone.

She burst into a fit of weeping and beckoned me over to a small stool set close to the head of her bed. I hurried to her and, although I was fighting back my own tears, tried to soothe her. It was some time, however, before she was able to speak and then she told her story in a broken whisper.

The first part of it I knew from what I had overheard the night before. What happened after that was almost more distressing, for the Prince, infuriated, dragged her back to her rooms and summoned her English attendants.

"They came in half asleep, wearing bedgowns and chamber robes," sobbed Mary. "And he raged at them— said that they were responsible for my outrageous behavior. Lisa, it was dreadful! I'll never forget it as long as I live. They just stood there, dumbfounded. I tried to speak, to tell William that it was not their fault at all, but he shouted at me to be quiet."

A burst of fresh tears intervened at this point and I did what I could to comfort her, saying that surely the Prince would seek her out soon and all would be well.

"No, no! He won't—I sent for him this morning and he refused to come. He won't speak to me! But I haven't told you the worst part, Lisa; he dismissed Anne Trelawney and my dear Mistress Langford and gave them only two hours to leave the palace. In the middle of the night!"

What could I say? I just sat there silently, waiting for her to go on.

"You must promise to stay with me, Lisa, you must! I have no one left now but the Villierses. The Villierses! After what happened last night! I can't bear to look at them." Clutching my hand with hot trembling fingers, she whispered directly into my ear. "I shall rid myself of that woman if it's the last thing I do—even if William never speaks to me again!"

∽

This was the beginning of a most unpleasant interval for us all. Whenever William dined or supped at the palace he sat beside his wife in icy silence, his whole attitude so repelling that she often left the high table in tears, and he did not set foot in her private apartments for two whole weeks. As his attitude toward me was unchanged I knew my part in their quarrel had escaped his notice, but the atmosphere at Court was so grim that I often longed to be somewhere else, I hardly cared where.

There were no more dancing evenings, of course, which spared me any encounters with Charles Seymour—a relief, in the circumstances. My cousin Harry returned to England soon after New Year's Day; he promised to keep me informed, and before long I received a letter from him saying that Thynne's case had not yet begun and that King Charles would write me himself.

My other serious concern—Carl's safety—was now set at rest by a bulletin from Tangiers: Carl, during an attack on the garrison there, had led a band of volunteers, gone on fighting after his horse was shot from under him, and had driven the Moors out of the fort and into the sea. It was a frightening tale, to be sure, but he was alive and well and the hero of the day.

With my own personal problems at a standstill, I turned all my energies to the task of cheering poor Mary. Nothing

I could say or do, however, raised her spirits, and I finally sought out William's aunt, the Princess of Oost Friesland, and begged her to intervene.

"I'll do what I can," she promised me, shaking her head. "It's usually a mistake to interfere in a matrimonial dispute, but I agree that this awkward, distressing situation has gone on far too long!"

I heard afterward that she told Prince William she would not leave The Hague until he made friends with his wife—and as her visit was already overlong and pressing business called her home, he reluctantly agreed to do what she asked.

Just how he did it, I do not know; Mary did not tell me and I, naturally, did not ask. But I do know that she changed, in one short hour, from a drooping, listless young woman to a laughing, singing, dancing princess, and I went to bed that night happier than I had been in months.

❧

I waked the following morning to find that the outside world had changed, too. For several days the weather had been turning colder, a heavy snowfall had begun shortly after midnight, lasting until dawn, the temperature had dropped another ten degrees, and the lake under our windows and all the canals were frozen solid.

When I joined Mary a few hours later, I found her deep in exciting plans. "William has been with me all morning," she said gaily, "and he's gone now to arrange a great snow carnival for tomorrow. We hold it most winters when the ice is solid enough; the schools and shops close and everyone for miles around skates into The Hague on the frozen canals to compete for money prizes that William offers for the best performances on the ice. He and I award the prizes in person, and then we put on our own skates and mingle with our people."

As she paused for breath, I marveled at the difference in her. "It sounds wonderful," I said. "I shall enjoy every minute of it."

"And that's not all," she went on, her eyes alight. "William is giving a supper and dancing party for us at his hunting lodge after the carnival. Imagine, Lisa—William! We'll drive there in sleighs and wear carnival costumes and masks. Our sleigh is a swan, all red and gold."

The childlike quality that Mary had never outgrown and that made her so lovable and appealing was very much in evidence, and I couldn't help laughing at her sudden enthusiasm. It was apparent that his Highness, having decided to forgive her, was now making a great effort to improve their relationship. I wondered what he would do about Betty Villiers and how long this would last, but I determined to do what I had just said to Mary—enjoy every minute of it.

❧

The weather was perfect for the snow carnival, and as far as I could tell everything else was perfect, too. It looked to me as if everybody in The Hague must be on the ice, rich, poor, young, old; those who were too stout or elderly for skates were pushed around in hand sledges, joining noisily in the fun.

Princess Mary, awarding her share of the prizes, was both charming and genuinely interested in the winners, and when she and William joined their people and skated here and there among the crowds, I could see that she was beloved by them all.

Our party then retired to the palace, where we donned

our costumes and masks, climbed into horse-drawn sleighs, and drove to Prince William's hunting lodge, some miles out in the country. It was a gay ride over the snowy roads, the hot supper waiting us in the rustic hall was appetizing, and the hour of dancing afterward more pleasant than I had thought possible with Mary's stern husband playing host.

Tonight he surprised us all by unbending for once; masked but unmistakable, he moved freely among us, chatting, laughing, even dancing with several of the ladies. Our other partners were not so easy to recognize, but soon after supper I was claimed by a hooded monk whose laugh and partly disguised voice sounded very much like Charles Seymour's.

It was all so delightful that I was sorry when the music stopped and we were told that the sleighs were waiting to take us back to The Hague. I saw William seat Mary himself, tucking a fur rug around her legs, then get in beside her. Their apparent felicity made me even happier, as did the announcement, just before we pulled out of the courtyard, that the evening's entertainment was not over; those who wished to skate on the lake before retiring could do so.

Here, too, Prince William had prepared for our comfort. Servants were ready to fasten on our skates and provide us with hot drinks, the lake was lighted by flares and bonfires, and the same musicians who had played while we danced appeared to play while we skated.

The moment my skates were strapped on, two young gallants scooped me up and led me out on the ice. All around us were couples or other threesomes. As I watched some of the ladies floundering around in voluminous skirts and elaborately trained gowns, I realized how fortunate I had been in my choice of costume. After trying on several, I had decided to wear the veils, leather boots, and ankle-length brocaded coat of a Persian noblewoman. The jeweled headband hid my red hair, the veils my face, and the boots and coat were ideal for skating.

With a young man holding me by each arm and my hands snug in a large fur muff, I glided boldly away from the bank, my unencumbered legs free to keep time to the music. As we laughed and sang and swooped around the softly lighted stretch of frozen water I forgot, for the moment, all my troubles. Tonight I was not Elizabeth Percy, Countess Ogle, Countess Carrots, or La Triste Héritière, a new title someone had given me; no, tonight I was a nameless Persian lady enjoying an exhilarating sport.

After several swift circles we were accosted by the hooded monk, who, by falsely and firmly claiming a previous commitment on my part, detached me from my two unknown companions and swung me off in the opposite direction. Neither of us said anything, but as he lengthened his stride and we seemed to fly over the ice I gave a little laugh of delight.

Then I suddenly sobered, remembering how Carl and I had skated together at Ightham Mote. How could I find so much pleasure now, with someone else? Anyone else?

My legs slowed involuntarily. Just as I was about to make some excuse and join the group of ladies on the bank keeping warm by one of the fires, another skater swooped down on us. He was a dim figure, at first, but a moment later I could see that he was tall, unmasked, and wearing a plain traveling cloak.

I think I stumbled. I remember Charles steadying me, then greeting the other man in friendly surprise. "Von Löwenhaupt, isn't it? When did *you* come back to The Hague?"

"Just tonight, too late to join your supper party. May I borrow your partner, my friend?"

With a laughing protest, Charles surrendered me to

Carl and skated off alone. Speechless, breathless, I clung to Carl with both hands, my legs trembling.

"Come," was all he said, but he held me in such a firm grip that my feet obeyed his, somehow, and we moved smoothly off together into a darker part of the lake.

"I couldn't stay away, my heart," he said then. "I had to come back to you. You *must* come away with me, Lisa, you *must.*"

I swallowed a sob and shook my head in the darkness. "I can't, Carl. I can't. The Court has decided that my marriage is legal, and Thomas Thynne is suing for marital restitution."

"So. Then I must free you in the only way left. I will challenge this Thynne and settle the matter. . . ."

17

I was about to retire when Mary slipped into my bed-chamber that night for a few minutes of private talk. She wanted to know, of course, what had passed between Carl and me.

"I told him where you were on the ice," she said, "and described your costume. Apparently he came right to the palace, hoping to find you."

At first, after I repeated the gist of our conversation, she seemed to think the threat of a duel a minor matter.

"Not this one," I assured her grimly. "Carl means it to be a fight to the death, and I believe him. He'll be in danger whichever way it goes, and I cannot allow it to take place. Help me, your Highness, please help me! He left me so abruptly tonight that I don't even know where he is staying or when he plans to leave The Hague. Send for him and make him promise not to do this mad thing!"

Realizing finally that my fears were justified, Mary agreed to do what I asked, and we both retired. I know that she sent someone to find Carl quite early the next morning, but despite the fact that The Hague is not a large city it was more than a week before we had any word of him.

Even in a small place it is not easy to trace a foreigner who has good reason for hiding his identity, and Carl had covered his tracks very cleverly. What we learned, however, was that he had not gone directly to England, which eased the worst of my anxieties; he had paid his debts here at The Hague and, accompanied by a man named Captain Vratz, had set out for Le Havre.

"Captain Vratz sounds like a soldier," I said to Mary. "Perhaps Carl is merely looking for fresh adventure. In any event, you have done all you can and I am truly grateful!"

"I wish I could do something to help poor Charles Seymour," was her reply. "I'm sorrier for him, Lisa, than I am for your Carl. After all, Carl knows you love him; Charles has nothing."

I flushed and fell silent.

"Well, I comfort myself with the thought that Charles is young enough to fall in love with someone else before too long," Mary went on. "He thinks he won't, of course, but I remember swearing to love my handsome Scot until I died and here I am caring only for the man they forced me to marry! Life is certainly queer."

That thought of Mary's that Charles would soon forget me did not, for some reason, comfort me as much as it should. But I called myself a dog in the manger, selfish and greedy, and tried to put the matter out of my mind by thinking instead of Mary's situation. She had lost some of her glow again.

"It's not William," she assured me. "It's Betty Villiers. She takes every opportunity to hurt me—nothing open, just little sneering remarks and digs. But this is something I must settle by myself. I have a plan which may work; I shan't tell you yet, Lisa, but I'm hoping to rid my life of her one of these days."

We said nothing more about our problems for there was little to say. It did no good to dwell on mine, and I was glad to know that there was no fresh quarrel between her and William. As for Charles, I had done everything I could to make him realize that he must forget me.

It was either the day after the snow carnival and William's masked supper party or the day after that when I received a note from the young Duke, asking me for a private interview. After a bit of indecision I agreed, suggesting that we meet in the pleasure grounds behind the palace. It was time, I told myself, to listen to whatever Charles had to say to me and to be quite honest with *him*, if I could. Harry thought he had warned Charles off; if he had failed, it was my duty to do so.

My choice of a meeting place was a good one. The snow had been swept from the paths so that Mary's entourage could walk there during the warmest part of the day if they wished; but I was almost sure that this extremely cold weather would keep everyone else indoors, and so it proved to be.

I tied on my warmest cloak, joined Charles at the appointed time and place, and for a few minutes we strolled around the brown flower beds, each, I suppose, trying to think of how to break the awkward silence.

"I—had to see you," said Charles at last. "I have just received a letter from London, telling me something I can't believe. I know it's just gossip—you *can't* be married to Thomas Thynne! Harry Sidney said Lady Percy was arranging another match for you, but you've been here the whole time. I wrote her myself, a few weeks ago, and begged her to give you to me, to change her plans, to listen to me—"

Before I could reply, he went on, his voice anguished.

"She has not answered me! And now I hear this incredible story!"

"It *is* incredible," I said. "But it is true, Charles." And I told him the whole sorry tale, ending with Carl's threat to call Thomas Thynne out on the field of honor.

"And now you see,"—I raised my head at last—"why only Princess Mary knows my secret. Or did know, I should say. To be such a fool, so easily duped—"

He was looking at me with such blazing eyes, such anger, that I stopped in mid-sentence and actually moved a few steps away, flinching as if he had struck me. I had never seen him anything but gentle and courteous, and this response frightened me. Was he jealous of Carl? Or hating me for keeping silent so long?

But almost before those questions formed in my mind he was at my side, bending over me. "No, no, Lisa, don't look like that. I'm not angry at *you*. It's Lady Percy I want to kill—with my bare hands, slowly! To force you into two such marriages, to ruin your life, to make you so desperately unhappy—she's worse than a murderess, a torturer. And your Carl hasn't made things any easier for you, either, you poor child."

I think I must have given a great sigh of relief, for he smiled down at me, took my arm, and walked me slowly up and down the path.

"There," he said, "that's better. I must not let you get too cold. Now, tell me what I can do to help."

His sudden thoughtfulness was almost harder to bear than his anger. "Oh, Charles." I shook my head at him, my voice breaking. "Don't be so kind to me! I'm afraid I've treated you very badly. But I didn't mean to, truly I didn't."

"Of course you didn't. Now stop worrying about *me*, Lisa. I don't want my love for you to spoil our friendship."

I often thought of that talk, comforted and reassured by Charles's sympathy and understanding. And when he remained at The Hague, meeting me always as if we were casual friends, I was soon able to enjoy his company again as much as I had in the past.

All seemed to be well, too, between William and Mary, and as a few peaceful weeks slipped away I almost forgot her threat to rid herself of his redheaded mistress. I thought she had, as well, until one morning in the middle of February when Prince William rode off to his hunting lodge for several days' sport.

This, it seemed, was what Mary was waiting for. First, I watched her struggling with a long letter; then I heard her summon Elizabeth Villiers to her presence chamber. I asked if I should retire, but she shook her head. "No, Lisa. Please stay."

It was some time before the usher brought Betty in; she had been, she said, with her sister Anne, who had recently wed one of William's ministers and was moving from the palace to a private house nearby.

Princess Mary listened to her excuses coldly, then indicated the paper on her desk. "I have here a most important letter," she told her lady-in-waiting, "that must be carried to England on tomorrow's packet boat and handed personally to my lord father. As you have not been home for more than a year, Lady Betty, and must be longing for a glimpse of your family, I have decided to entrust this errand to you."

I saw Betty look at her with instant suspicion, her nostrils flaring slightly, her eyes wary. Without a moment's hesitation, she stated several reasons why she could not obey Mary's order: she had been feeling rather unwell, Anne needed her help in settling into her new house, and some urgent personal business made this a bad time for her to leave The Hague.

Mary replied to each objection in turn, restraining her temper with difficulty. "My own doctor will examine you, Lady Betty, and determine whether you are too ill to travel. I am sure that your sister will agree that my affairs come before hers, and I am certain you can arrange that urgent business of your own in time to sail tomorrow."

"I'm afraid not, your Highness," said Lady Betty insolently. "I forgot to add that Prince William asked me to entertain the new Spanish minister while he is away, and I have invited him to dine with me tomorrow. In the circumstances, I must ask you to send someone else."

I held my breath and kept my head bent over the fine linen shirt Mary and I were making for the Prince. If Betty wanted to remain in Holland she had just made a fatal mistake. Mary would not sit down under that last insulting excuse.

"I have always understood," I heard Mary say in icy tones, "that you were a member of my suite, not Prince William's. I will, I assure you, be more than happy to explain to my husband the reason for your absence and for your failure to carry out his wishes. Go to your rooms immediately, Lady Elizabeth. My physician will come to you there within the hour and, if he finds nothing seriously amiss, I command you to prepare for your journey. I will provide you with an escort to see you safely aboard the packet, and I want it clearly understood, madam, that you must not leave either your apartments or the palace until you set out for England."

Almost spitting with anger, but unable to make any further protest, Betty sketched a curtsy and backed out.

"There!" said Mary firmly. "Now she knows who is mistress here!" Summoning a lackey to her side, she ordered him to stand guard in the corridor outside Lady Elizabeth's chambers. "Bring me any letters she wishes despatched," she said, "and come to me if she tries to leave the palace."

This done, she turned to me and explained the rest of her plan. "That letter to my father asks him to keep Betty in England from now on," she told me. "So pray for favorable winds, Lisa. That packet must sail tomorrow!"

It did, and Betty Villiers sailed with it. To celebrate, and to stop thinking of what William might say about all this, Mary sent for her musicians and arranged for an evening's dancing. We were neither of us surprised to see Charles Seymour arrive with the other foreign visitors and I was, in fact, just finishing a pleasant dance with him when one of the royal servants approached me, holding a thick letter on a silver salver.

"I beg your pardon, milady," he said, "but a courier brought this to the palace. I believe it is for you."

Startled, I took it. It was addressed in a strange hand to "Mistress Thomas Thynne, formerly the Lady Ogle."

Charles, beside me, asked if anything was wrong.

"I don't know," I answered slowly, still staring at the address on the letter "I don't know." My first thought was that it might be from Thomas Thynne, my second that it was some formal notification of his lawsuit.

Shivering a little, I excused myself to Charles, tore it open, and read it. I must have turned white, for Charles instantly sprang to my side, led me to a bench in the nearest anteroom, and forced my head down between my knees.

"For God's sake, Lisa," he said urgently, "tell me what is the matter."

My head had stopped swimming. I held the letter out to him in a shaking hand. "Read it, Charles," I told him. "Read it! It says Thomas Thynne has been murdered in cold blood and they're going to arrest Carl."

18

Charles merely glanced at the paper I gave him; then, with a muffled oath, he raised me to my feet. "Come," he said. "I'll take you to your woman and ask Princess Mary to go to you as soon as she can."

I was still so shaken that I obeyed him without saying a word, grateful to be told what to do, and when I reached my apartments I sat down in the nearest chair and waited, numbly, for Mary. This fresh horror was too much for me to even think about alone; as it was, I had to put my head down every little while to keep from fainting.

Dolly fussed around me, holding a vial of salts under my nose whenever she saw me bend over, giving me sips of wine and urging me to lie down on my bed. But I refused, thinking it best to stay where I was until Mary came.

After what seemed like hours the door opened and she hurried in, followed by Charles.

"Mother of God, Lisa," she exclaimed, almost running to my side. "Can this possibly be true?"

"I don't know," I replied. "I don't know."

Charles picked up the packet and brought it to us. "Perhaps we should read all of this now, Lisa," he suggested. "Do you feel well enough?"

"Now that you two are here with me, I do," I said, trying to smile. "I was so shocked by that first letter I hardly noticed there were other things with it."

We all moved to a table, Dolly lighted working candles for us, and we spread the package of papers over it. There were several letters, we saw, and some sheets of newsprint. We began reading them, speaking occasionally as we did so.

Mary held up one of the pieces of newspaper and read a bit of it in a horrified voice: " 'On the evening of February twelfth, returning home from a visit to the Countess of Northumberland'—That's your grandmother, Lisa. How ghastly this all is! It says here Thynne lived until morning and that the leader of the assassins was a Captain Vratz. Isn't that the name of the man who was with Carl when he left The Hague?"

"I think it was," I admitted reluctantly. "But there must be some mistake. Carl told me he was going to challenge Mr. Thynne to a duel. He would never be a party to this kind of crime!"

"But it says here that three Swedish soldiers, supposedly in the employ of Count Königsmark, stopped Thomas Thynne's coach on Pall Mall and one of them shot him with a blunderbuss." Mary looked at me, paused, and turned to Charles.

"What is in those two letters?" she asked him.

"They're from King Charles and Harry Sidney, confirming this grim business, I'm sorry to say, and advising Lisa to remain here with you until it's cleared up."

"Cleared up?"

He nodded. "They've arrested Vratz and two other men

named Stern and Borosky. Borosky did the actual shooting. And they're hunting for Königsmark as an accessory before the fact; the other three are to be tried for murder, apparently."

Mary shuddered and picked up the last letter. "This seems to be from a cousin of Thomas Thynne," she said, reading it swiftly. "Asking what you want done about the funeral."

"Asking *me*?" I could hear my voice rise, then break. "Me? How could anyone think I would care?"

"It must be someone who doesn't know the circumstances of your marriage and thinks that as his widow—"

"His widow?" I gave a sudden hysterical laugh. "Why, so I am. Now everyone will point at me again and say that I'm a 'maid, wife, and widow' twice over!"

Charles broke in hurriedly. "Harry and the King are right, Lisa. You must stay here until this whole dreadful matter is over with and forgotten. Go to bed now—have a hot posset to help you sleep—and we'll discuss this again when we know more about it." He rose and looked down at me. "And remember, whether you want me to or not, I shall stay here too for a while, hoping that I can help in some way."

~

Three days later, three days that seemed like a hundred years to me, another courier arrived at the palace, this time bringing me a letter from my grandmother. I opened it with trembling fingers, dreading whatever might be in it— and, I soon saw, with good reason.

It was nasty and vindictive; every word was meant to hurt me. This whole disgraceful affair, she said, was my fault and I well deserved the misery it entailed. Because I had run away and incited a villain to commit murder, a good man was dead and the Percy name dragged in the dirt. At least three necks would be stretched, she went on, and her one hope was that the guilty Königsmark, whom she had spotted as a ruthless adventurer and fortune hunter at first sight, would be caught and dangle with them. As proof of the shame I had brought on our family she was enclosing a batch of ballads and broadsides rushed into print by the scurvy rogues in Grub Street.

"If her Highness is fool enough to keep you with her in the face of all this," she finished, "stay where you are. I go to Petworth this very day as I can no longer endure the malicious faces and tongues here in London."

"I am more than 'fool enough,'" said Mary when I showed her the letter. "I am *glad* you are here, Lisa, glad!"

My eyes filled with grateful tears and I gave her a kiss. "Hearing you say so is comforting," I told her, "but read these broadsides. Here, this one claims that Thomas Thynne shot himself for love of me, his runaway wife; this one says Mistress Trevor was the murderess; and these last three all accuse *me* of the crime. I hired a 'band of foreign bravos' to rid myself of a husband I detested, apparently."

"Disgusting!" was Mary's instant response. "Forget them, Lisa. No one ever believes that kind of filth."

"Perhaps not," I agreed, "but in a way I *am* responsible for the whole thing. If I hadn't allowed my grandmother to trick me into that marriage, none of this would have happened. Because of my stupidity, one man is dead and at least three more will die! Perhaps Carl—I can't just stay here and wait for him to be hanged. You must see that."

"I know it's hard, Lisa, but what else can you do?"

"Go home and help to clear him. I *know* he is innocent. I *know* it!" Then, seeing her look at me with pitying eyes, I tried to reassure her. "You must not worry about me any more. I have it all planned. I'll take Dolly and cross on the next packet boat. If I wear a plain gown and cloak no one will pay the least attention to me, and when I reach London I'll go right to Lady Temple."

❧

Two days later Dolly and I were snugly ensconced in a small private sitting room in the Angel Inn at Helversluys, waiting for the packet boat to sail. Princess Mary, finally realizing that all her protests and arguments were useless, had sent us there on one of the royal barges and had despatched a servant earlier to engage one of the two cabins on the ship.

It had not been easy to say farewell, even with this thoughtful assistance, and now, as Dolly and I sat together at a small table nibbling at cheese and the inevitable pickled herring, I began to feel a little frightened. It had taken all my faltering Dutch and my faltering courage to hire the room and order the meal, and the thought of the journey facing me and the grim troubles waiting in England made me want to run right back to Princess Mary.

A scratch at the door brought me to my feet. Who could that be?

Dolly hurried over and opened it. There, smiling at me, stood Charles Seymour, clad in plain breeches, a long stuff coat, and with a traveling cloak folded over his arm.

"Charles! What in heaven's name are *you* doing here?"

"Waiting to sail on the packet boat," he replied calmly, stepping inside.

"Oh, that Mary! This is her doing, I know it is!"

"Well, she did tell me you were leaving today, and we both agreed that as you were traveling incognito there was no reason why I should not cross on the same boat and keep an eye on you. No one will know, Lisa. I've looked at the list of passengers and they're all strangers."

"And where is your tutor?"

Looking a bit guilty, Charles admitted that he'd slipped away, leaving a note. "He'll settle our affairs at The Hague and follow in a few days."

By the time we were on board and Dolly was helping me disrobe for the night, I admitted to myself that Charles's presence was a great comfort. He'd remained carefully in the background while we were claiming our cabin, but I knew he was there to help if we needed him. And I had, after a short argument, given him permission to arrange our journey from Harwich to London—and to accompany us.

Dolly tucked me into the shelflike bed and ventured out, returning with a cup of steaming hot chocolate for me. While I sipped it, she said the steward had commented on my hair, saying that they had had another red-haired lady who had made the trip to Harwich and then returned on the next crossing.

I think I sat up abruptly; I know I slopped some chocolate on the tray. "She returned?" I almost said the name "Betty Villiers" out loud, but I caught myself and made some vague comment instead.

❧

I slept well, being exhausted, and favorable winds took us to Harwich on schedule. Charles, leaving us in the Amsterdam, the cleanest of the town's inns, proceeded to hire a comfortable coach, four horses, and two outriders, and we were soon on our way. The roads, we were glad to find, were in fair condition; England had not had the heavy snows that had blanketed Holland, nor the freezing weather, and as a result we were able to reach London before midnight.

We drove slowly along Pall Mall, watching for the Temples' house. The spot where Thomas Thynne had been shot to death, must be nearby; the very thought made my flesh crawl. Charles, understanding as always, said little until we reached our destination.

Then, as one of our outriders pounded on the Temples' door, he turned to me. "Shall I come in with you and explain matters to Lady Temple?"

"Please, no," I replied, shaking my head. "My appearance will be disturbing enough without the need to tell her this is not an elopement!"

"I wish it were."

"I shouldn't have said that. Forgive me, Charles, and thank you for everything—everything!" On impulse, I found his hand in the darkness and for the space of a heartbeat held it to my cheek. "My dear friend," I said. "My very dear friend!"

As she had that day at Sheen, Lady Temple welcomed me with open arms. This time, of course, I did not need to tell her of the fresh disasters that had overtaken me; she and all London knew more about Thomas Thynne's murder than I did.

I expected a scolding for returning to England and, although I received one, it was mild; when I explained that I felt I must come to help Carl prove his innocence, she merely sighed and shook her head.

She was more outspoken about the part Charles Seymour played in my journey home. "I recognize Princess Mary's romantic hand in this," she said. "I'm glad you had someone to look after you on the way over, but sending young Seymour to act as courier could have led to more gossip and problems for you. It might still, Lisa, and if he calls here I shall have to send him about his business."

The next day Harry Sidney dropped in to see me, having heard from Lady Temple of my arrival.

"Dear Harry!" I greeted him warmly, kissing him on both cheeks. "You always appear when I need you most!"

"I hardly need say that you should not have appeared at all. This is very naughty of you, Lisa, and I can only hope the King will not be too angry. He told you to remain in The Hague, and you certainly should have obeyed him."

"I know," I admitted, "but I *had* to come home, Harry, and I want to see his Majesty just as soon as possible to tell him why. I know Carl can't be guilty—I'm sure those men made some kind of a mistake! I must help clear him, Harry, I must. I'm certain King Charles will believe me when I assure him that Carl will come forward soon and explain everything."

Instead of replying, he merely looked at me, his face filled with pity.

"He *will*, Harry," I insisted passionately. "Of course he will!"

"I'm afraid not, Lisa," he said now. "I hate to be the one to tell you this, but Königsmark was arrested two nights ago in very suspicious circumstances. Another few hours and it would have been too late; he was preparing to flee the country."

"No, no," I protested vehemently, "he was probably seeking proof of his innocence. If they'd given him time—"

"He had time and to spare." His words and his quiet tones made my heart sink. "He had seven days, my dear child—seven full days. And when they caught him at last he was at Gravesend, in disguise, having just paid his passage on a Swedish ship that was to sail the following morning."

While I sought desperately for some new excuse, Harry went on talking.

"I must tell you, too," he went on, "that King Charles

was present when his council questioned the three men who were involved in the actual shooting, and he says the picture is very black indeed."

When I asked Harry what he meant by "very black," he said that the murderers had told a wild story that they assumed was justification for the shooting. That Thomas Thynne insulted Carl, refused to meet him on the field of honor, then sent six hired desperadoes to France to kill *him*; that in this attack on him Carl was twice wounded but escaped after killing two of Thynne's men. And after that Carl decided he must protect his own life by doing away with Thynne.

I looked at Harry in bewilderment. Could anyone believe such a tale? Or was I too upset to understand it? Carl had told me that he would kill Thomas Thynne in a duel to free me, but all the rest of it sounded ridiculous.

"It's all lies, of course," Harry went on. "I've heard that Königsmark accused Thynne of tricking you into marriage and threatened to brand him a coward unless he set a time and place for a duel. I can believe *that*, and I can believe that when Thynne refused, your Carl decided to free you in another way."

"Then it is all my fault, Harry. I should have done something to prevent this."

"If we go back far enough," said Harry, "we can blame Lady Percy and Thynne. But that doesn't help now, I'm sorry to say. I don't know anything that will help now."

"Could you arrange for me to see Carl, to talk to him?"

"Good God, Lisa! Do you want to put the rope right around his neck?" He stared at me in horror. "Carl's only hope is to prove he did not have Thynne killed in order to marry you."

I will not attempt to describe the agony I lived through while we all waited for Carl and the other three men to come to trial. I remained quietly with Lady Temple for a few days; then, at the insistence of the King, I moved to Northumberland House. There would be less talk, he said, if I were residing under a Percy roof; at his "suggestion," Lady Percy would stay down at Petworth until the trial was over, and Lady Lucy Hay joined me in London as companion and duenna.

As I did not have to endure my grandmother's presence, I was not sorry to do as King Charles wished. Much as I loved Lady Temple, much as I loved Princess Mary, I was tired of being a visitor, and during these weeks of anxiety and unhappiness it was a relief to live in the seclusion of my own apartments, be waited on by my own servants, and pass the dragging hours with no need to consider anyone but myself. Lady Lucy understood just how I was feeling and, as usual, made no demands on me.

I did see Lady Temple from time to time, of course, and my cousin Harry, but all other visitors were denied admittance. There was no one else I wanted to talk to, no one else I *could* talk to with any ease. And even talking to those two good friends was not always a pleasure—for them or for me.

Poor Harry, I know, must have dreaded many of our interviews, for it was usually his task to bring me what news there was. And when he announced that the date of the trial had been set, he had to listen to a barrage of pleading and arguments that made us both weary before it was over.

I remember him rising, at last, and shaking his head grimly at me. What I wanted, of course, was to attend the trial. I will never know how I finally persuaded him to take me, but I did. When we set out for Old Bailey, Harry was still protesting that he must be mad to have agreed to such a thing.

As we neared the double doors that led into the courtroom I heard a sonorous voice, going on and on.

"Quick!" I said. "They've begun!"

I saw my cousin Harry exchange a patient look with Lady Lucy and step over to the guard, say a word or two, and hand him a coin.

"We've missed nothing, Lisa," he reassured me. "They've chosen the jury, and Sir Francis Winnington has begun his opening speech. Everything he says will be gone through again later in detail, but come along; the guard has saved the seats I reserved for you."

Once inside, Harry, his head carefully averted, settled us on a bench high up in the spectators' gallery. "Here you are," he whispered. "Don't forget to keep your hoods down around your faces." Then, as we knew he must, he moved away and left us there. Too many people might recognize him and, if he remained with me, guess my identity.

When he was gone I looked first at the dark, rather shriveled face of the judge. He was listening intently to Winnington, one hand playing with his pen, the other resting on his gavel. My eyes, after that, found the enclosure where the prisoners sat, but my view was blocked by a tall man sitting on the bench in front of me. Then I saw a mirror on the ceiling over the enclosure which gave me a sudden startling glimpse of Carl's gleaming golden head and a flash of bright blue as he raised his head to stare at the Solicitor General.

A moment later I heard Sir Francis mention Carl's name, and I made myself concentrate on what the red-faced elderly man in the black robes, white linen bands, and worn white periwig was telling the Court. At first it seemed to be a muddle of lodgings, Polanders, blunderbusses, confessions, and issues; then my confused senses cleared and every word reached me.

"Count Königsmark," he said, "is a gentleman of great quality, such quality that I am extremely sorry to find the evidence against him so strong. I wish, in fact, that his innocence were greater and the evidence in my brief less, but there seems little doubt but that he was the main abettor and arranger of this barbarous business. This we shall prove on these grounds:"

As he paused, either to take breath or to underline the drama of the moment, I tried to see Carl again in the glass. This time I had a second or two in which to study his whole face. It was so expressionless, so impassive, that it could have been the face of a stranger.

"First"—now the Solicitor General began to count off the points against Carl, his voice ringing out in the quiet room—"first, we know that he had designs on Mr. Thynne's life. For, gentlemen"—swinging around, he spoke directly to the jury—"when he came to England about three weeks before the murder he assumed a disguise, hid himself in a remote part of the city, and frequently moved his lodgings from place to place.

"*Then*"—he emphasized the word strongly—"he sent someone to find out from the Swedish Envoy whether he could legally marry the Lady Ogle if he had first killed Mr. Thynne in a duel, which makes it obvious that his plan was somehow to effect Mr. Thynne's death."

I heard Lady Lucy gasp and I was, myself, so horrified and shocked that I missed what he said next. I could understand Carl rushing to England in a fit of desperation and calling Thynne out, but to behave in this coldblooded manner made me feel as if something loathsome had walked over my heart, leaving a trail of slime.

A stir in the courtroom and the loud voice of the usher calling the first witness for the Crown roused me. It was one of Thynne's servants, summoned to give his account of the crime.

"My master," he began, "was coming home from the Countess of Northumberland's. I had a flambeau in my hand and was walking ahead of our coach when I heard the blunderbuss go off. I turned around, saw a great cloud of smoke, and heard my master cry out that he was murdered. There were three horsemen riding away on the right side of the coach; I ran after them, shouting 'Murder! Murder!' until I was too much out of breath to run any farther."

"Look upon the prisoners at the bar," ordered the Prosecutor formally. "Can you swear any or all of them were the men?"

"I cannot, my lord. I did not see their faces."

Soon after that he was excused, and Thynne's coachman took his place on the stand. His story was even more terrible.

"My lord," he said, "I was driving my master from my

Lady Northumberland's house. When we neared St. Alban's Street three men rode up to the right side of the coach; one of them shouted 'Stop, you dog!' and, as I looked around, they fired right into the coach at my master and ran away as fast as they could."

"Are the men at the bar the persons you saw?"

"I cannot say they were, my lord."

The shooting now having been established, the Crown called a Mr. Hobbs, the surgeon who attended Mr. Thynne, and the Coroner. Each in turn testified to the nature and extent of the wounds and injuries, going into such detail that a wave of nausea swept over me and Lady Lucy, sitting quietly beside me, looked quite green.

I could understand now why Harry had been so reluctant to bring us here today, why I had had to beg and plead.

I pulled my hood farther over my face and swallowed hard. A moment later the Prosecutor began questioning the first of the three main defendants, the man named Borosky who, it was said, had done the actual shooting. As he neither spoke nor understood English, two interpreters were summoned; with their help, Sir Francis soon induced the prisoner to admit that he had indeed fired the blunderbuss at Thomas Thynne. Captain Vratz gave him the gun, he said, and ordered him to shoot Thynne as soon as they stopped the coach.

While Captain Vratz was taking his place in the box, the man who had blocked my view of Carl rose and left the gallery. I could see Carl very clearly now, and as Vratz's questioning began I watched him closely, expecting to see the emotion he must be feeling for his friend. It was for his sake that Captain Vratz was here, facing the gallows—a dreadful burden for Carl to bear, surely.

But I still saw nothing. Even when Vratz took the blame for the shooting on his own shoulders, insisting that

Thynne had insulted Count Königsmark and that he, Vratz, determined to avenge that insult himself without informing Carl, not a muscle moved in Carl's face.

Surely, I thought, Carl will say something! He can't just sit there and let this happen. But he could. Before long it was proven without a shadow of a doubt that Thynne had never insulted Carl in any way and that Vratz had never met Thynne or spoken to him. Still Carl said nothing.

"But we sent Thynne challenges," said Captain Vratz, "and he disregarded them!"

"It is the custom in your country," asked Sir Francis, "to shoot a man if he won't fight?"

The testimony of Stern, the third man in the shooting affray, was equally damaging to the defense. He had confessed, originally, that Captain Vratz had offered him three or four hundred crowns to find a man willing to kill Thomas Thynne; if he could hire an Italian to do it, Vratz promised to provide two poniards for that purpose.

Now Stern, under oath, denied this; but I could see that the jury looked skeptical and I myself doubted that the Prosecution would invent such a detailed story.

None of the defendants had cleared himself in any way, and when they next called Sir John Reresby, who was responsible for the apprehension and indictment of all four prisoners, I could see no hope for them.

I grew weary, as Sir John went over the now familiar ground; weary, heartsick, frightened, and ashamed. It must be Carl's turn soon; I wondered how I could bear it.

But they did not summon Carl when Sir John stepped down; instead they opened the case against him by calling a man named Frederic Hanson. He was a grizzled middle-aged gentleman, wearing a coat and breeches of foreign cut, and he carried himself with an air of authority.

At first he said he was a friend of Carl's and had known

him for four years. Later he admitted that he was young
Philip's tutor and traveling companion, employed by Carl
to look after his brother.

His testimony went something like this: Soon after Carl
returned to England, he sent Hanson a letter written in his
own hand but signed "Carlo Cusk." He visited Carl in several lodging houses; Carl moved often, rarely left his chambers, was known to his lodging keepers as 'Stranger,' and
saw no one but himself, Captain Vratz, and a Dr. Frederick.

"Did you carry any messages from the Count to the
Swedish Envoy?"

For the first time the witness hesitated and dropped his
eyes, his hands moving nervously on the rail of the box.

"Well, my lord," he replied at last, "Count Königsmark
never ordered me to go to the Swedish Envoy, but he did
say he would like his advice. So when I felt obliged to go
and pay my respects to the Envoy, for he had treated me
and Count Philip very civilly before, I remembered this
conversation and mentioned the business."

"What was the business? What was Königsmark's message to the Envoy?"

"There was no direct message, my lord. Count Carl said
to me—in private talk, you understand—that Esquire
Thynne had used abusive language about him and he
wanted to know what the consequences would be if he
called him to account. Knowing that he wanted the Envoy's opinion, I asked him, as I have said, and received this
answer: If the Count should in any way meddle with
Thynne he would have a bad living in England. The Envoy
could not answer as to the law in this particular case, but
he would inquire into it. However, I never spoke to him
again."

"Remember that you are under oath and that you have

been questioned about this before," warned Sir Francis sternly. "Now tell me, did you ever hear the Count speak of fighting with Mr. Thynne?"

Hanson pursed up his mouth and looked vaguely over the Prosecutor's wigged head.

"Count Königsmark spoke to me in German," he said. "I spoke to the Swedish Envoy in French, and when I was before the King and the Council I spoke in English; and so I hope no one will, in the circumstances, put any evil construction on my words. I cannot remember the Count speaking of killing or dueling. I can swear he never told me he was resolved to fight Mr. Thynne or call him to account. If he said"—he stressed the little word—"*If* he should call him to account, what would be the consequences of it?"

"Call him to account for what?" Sir Francis was becoming impatient.

"Mr. Thynne had spoken abusively—reflected on the Count's person and on his horse."

A wave of laughter swept the spectators, and a man beside me gave an incredulous snort. The jurymen, too, were smiling at each other in amused disbelief.

One of the younger lawyers stood up. "Was there anything in that message to the Envoy about marrying my Lady Ogle?"

Here it was at last. Would this man continue to evade or would he deny this charge in a way that I could believe? Would he evade again, or would he give me back some of my faith in the man I loved?

"Well," admitted Hanson, "that was the last part of the Count's question. If he *should* meddle with Thynne, how would he stand in the eye of the English law in regard to his hopes concerning Lady Ogle?"

My heart sank. Then, as the questioning continued, with Hanson still hiding behind his excuse of discussing the matter in so many languages that he could not determine what had been said or meant, the Judge finally leaned down and spoke to Sir Francis Winnington.

"It grows late, my lord, and you make little progress with this witness. Let us recess for dinner and try again."

20

In the middle of the ensuing bustle and chatter, Harry Sidney's servant appeared and led Lady Lucy and me out of the courtroom and across the street to a small tavern. The low-ceiled common room was already crowded to the doors, but the innkeeper sent us up a steep staircase and into a tiny square parlor, lighted by a bulging old casement window and cheered by a fire of flaming logs.

Harry Sidney stepped forward as we entered and settled us at a table loaded with an appetizing array of dishes and platters.

"Go below, Corwin," he said to his servant, "and see about your own dinner. I'll wait on the ladies."

Turning to a side table, he poured out two tall goblets of red wine and handed them to us. "Here," he ordered. "You are both white and weary. Don't say a word until you've drunk this and had something to eat."

He reached for a knife and indicated the platters. "What will it be, my dears? Beef, mutton, eel pie? A little of everything?"

Lady Lucy shuddered. "I'm still queasy from all that talk about what the blunderbuss did to Mr. Thynne's insides. I don't believe I can swallow a mouthful."

"Nonsense!" was Harry's answer, and he proceeded to pile high three plates. Then, while we sipped our wine and began to eat a bit, he told us the very unusual history of the presiding judge, Chief Justice Pemberton. He was a complete rake as a youth, Harry said, consorting with lewd company, and so extravagant that he was finally thrown in debtor's prison. There, instead of frittering away the years, he busied himself studying the law, and when he was released he rose rapidly to the top of his new profession.

I suspect Harry was giving us time to recover from the morning's strains; I know that before long I felt much better myself and I saw that Lady Lucy had regained much of her color.

When he finished his story about the judge my eyes met his. They were looking at me with affection, understanding, and pity.

"This is an ugly business, child," he said to me gently, "and it will be even uglier before the day is over. Haven't you endured enough? Come, be sensible and let me send you home. I'll stay to the end for you and tell you all that happens."

I shook my head. "Please, no, Harry. I must hear Carl explain those terrible charges against him. I want to know the truth; you can see that, can't you?" Then a thought struck me. "They *will* let him speak, won't they?"

"Eventually, yes. But not before they've questioned all the people who saw him since his return to London: the lodging keepers and servants, the shopkeepers who sold him his disguises, the watermen at Rotherhithe—"

"Oh, dear," groaned Lady Lucy, dismayed. "All that, Harry? I'm so tired!"

"Let me go back to the courtroom by myself," I suggested. "And send Cousin Lucy home. Please, Harry. I'll be quite all right there in the gallery. No one has taken the slightest notice of us, and there are plenty of other women sitting there."

"Certainly not," replied Harry, and I could tell there was no use in trying any more persuasion. "I cannot possibly allow that, Lisa. However, let us do this: Königsmark will not be called to the stand until the other witnesses have testified and the Crown has summed up its case. If you and Lucy will remain here and rest, I promise faithfully to send Corwin to fetch you in plenty of time to hear both the summing up and Carl's defense. You don't need to hear everything twice, Lisa. For God's sake, spare yourself and Lucy that much!"

I must confess that I was secretly relieved. "You're very kind to me, Harry," I added, after agreeing to his proposal. "How can I ever thank you?"

"By being sensible, my dear. By opening your eyes and ears to the truth, however much it hurts. That's why I brought you here, you know—to do what you say you want, to know the truth. But that's enough preaching. Have some of this fruit tart. It looks delicious."

❧

After Harry left us, we watched the cheerful tavern maid whisk away the remains of our meal and then we both settled down to rest in chairs drawn close to the fire. Lady Lucy fell asleep almost immediately, her head on a soft pillow provided by the willing serving wench, but I was not so fortunate.

I could not stop thinking of the stories we had heard that morning; I could not forget Carl's impassive face, so like and yet so unlike the face of the man I loved; I heard Sir

Francis Winnington's voice, over and over in my ears, sharp, probing, relentless. And I saw each of the jurors in turn: curious, incredulous, fascinated, horrified, with mouths often actually agape.

Shivering, I reached my hands out to the fire. After a moment I rose and moved on quiet feet to the window. There was little to see, however, in the alley below: a cat munching a fish head, a shabby boy sweeping the tavern steps, the pleasant serving maid with a tankard in her hand, crossing the cobbles to a squat house with a heavy oaken door.

An hour dragged away. The shabby boy slipped in, piled more wood on the fire, and scrambled out. Lady Lucy opened her eyes, sighed, closed them again, and began to snore.

I walked up and down, trying to control my thoughts, my fingers twisted together so tightly that my knuckles turned white. What was happening in the courtroom? Would Corwin never come for us? Why had I agreed to remain here and suffer like this?

Another hour chimed on the small bracket clock. Then the door opened at last! I snatched up my cloak, sprang to Lady Lucy's side, and shook her awake.

∽∾

As we found our seats and sat down I heard Sir Francis say, his voice sounding very weary, "And that is the evidence for the Crown."

He turned his head toward Carl, the contrast between his odd face, lighted by a beam of late afternoon sun, and Carl's handsome features seeming almost ludicrous. "You have heard the evidence against you," he said. "It is charged that you were an accessory to the murder of Thomas Thynne, that you were the person who planned it and directed it. You have heard it sworn to that you came to England a fortnight or so before Thynne's death and that Captain Vratz, one of the three men who killed him, came here with you and stayed in your lodging."

He cleared his throat and continued. "It is charged that you used false names and shifted your lodging from time to time; that Borosky was brought over to England in compliance with your orders; that he came to your rooms and was provided by you with clothing and a sword. It has been asserted that you discussed with Mr. Hanson the possibility of calling out Mr. Thynne, wanting to know what the Swedish Envoy's opinion would be concerning it in relation to marrying Lady Ogle. It is further charged that Borosky spent the night preceding the murder with you, and that Captain Vratz came to you immediately the deed was done."

At this point in his summation I began to shake from head to foot and my stomach seemed tied in a quivering knot. It was worse, much worse than I had imagined it might be. Carl, Carl, I asked myself, how could you do these things? How could you?

But still the Chief Justice's voice went on and on, every word another nail in the coffin of my hopes.

"You left that lodging still incognito," I heard him say to Carl, "hiding your hair under a periwig. Your servant carried your clothes one way, while you went another to a secret lodging kept by a Swede at Rotherhithe. Here you disguised yourself as a jeweler and spent the time before embarking at Gravesend to flee England by being rowed around the river."

He looked directly at Carl, his eyes somber. "I must remind you that when you were taken you asked if Captain Vratz had confessed. You showed concern at the news that Borosky had admitted his guilt, and you said to the arresting officer, 'My lord, this is a stain on my name, but one good action in the wars will wash it clean.'"

In the grim silence that followed, I began to feel mercifully numb, almost as if my heart were encased in ice. But when Carl began to testify, a moment later, a dull pain penetrated the numbness and everything he said made it worse. For even to me, who loved him so well, his answers to the charges against him were false and unconvincing.

"I heard that there was to be an alliance between England, Sweden, and Holland against France," he said first, "so I came here to raise a regiment for King Charles. I remained in seclusion—incognito, if you prefer—because I had a rash on my arms and breast and did not want to go into company until it had healed. I left my first lodging because it was too cold, my second because the chimney smoked."

"And Borosky—why did you send for him?"

"To dress our horses the German way and to help purchase them. I had sent my young brother a thousand pistoles for that purpose."

"Had you any quarrel with Thomas Thynne? Did you, in fact, know him?"

Carl's eyes fell. "No, my lord, I did not."

"Then I ask you this: Did you, before coming back to England, hear that Mr. Thynne had married Lady Ogle?"

I felt Lady Lucy stir beside me as I waited for his answer.

"I did not hear of it, my lord, until I was in Strasbourg. All the town was discussing it there."

I looked at him with blind, horrified eyes. Carl had known of my marriage for weeks before going to Strasbourg. This obvious lie swept away my last feeble hope that he could clear himself, that he was somehow caught in a web spun by someone else. I realized now that his whole defense was made up of evasions, half-truths, and palpable

falsehoods. In fact, he was not really answering the charges
at all.

When he finished at last and the lawyers made their
final speeches, I studied the faces of the jury, trying to guess
what they were thinking. Their expressions changed very
little until the lawyers finished and the judge directed their
attention to a few points of law.

"When one man shoots another," he told them, "and
the two with him have come on purpose to aid him in the
crime, they are all guilty. The most doubtful question for
you, gentlemen, concerns Count Königsmark. Did he command, or give any authority, or direct that the murder be
done? Or did Captain Vratz, without the Count's knowl-
edge, decide to avenge his master's honor?

"If it is the latter, the law would not consider Count
Königsmark guilty. This is the crux of the matter, and this,
gentlemen of the jury, you must decide for yourself. Go,
and do your duty."

The clock on the wall ticked on in the darkening courtroom. It was late, very late. Fifteen minutes passed and my
head began to throb, but it was nothing to the ache in my
heart.

Thirty minutes—a rustle, an excited whisper, footsteps!
The jury was returning. Silence, tense silence fell. Then:

"Gentlemen, are you all agreed on your verdict?"

"We are."

"George Borosky, hold up your hand. Gentlemen of the
jury, look upon the prisoner. How say you? Is he guilty or
not guilty?"

"Guilty."

"Christopher Vratz, hold up your hand. Guilty or not
guilty?"

"Guilty."

"John Stern, hold up your hand. Guilty or not guilty?"

"Guilty."

"Carl John Königsmark, hold up your hand. Guilty or not guilty?"

"Not guilty."

I gasped, engulfed by a flood of relief. Then, as the Chief Justice reached for his black cap, I suddenly felt I could not bear to hear the end of this horrible business. I pulled at Lady Lucy's arm, and we slipped together up the aisle and out of the courtroom.

We found our coach and waited inside it for Harry to join us. Neither of us said a word; there was nothing to say.

He climbed in, after a few minutes, and the coach moved off toward Charing Cross.

"Well, my dear?" he said, taking my hand in his. "Are you happier now?"

I looked right into his eyes and shook my head. "Relieved, of course, that Carl won't hang—but not happier, Harry, not happier. How could I be when I know that he is guilty? The jury was wrong, Harry. Carl *should* hang!"

I read over what I had written, made a grimace of disgust, and tore it up. I tried again, and although I did not like it much better I sprinkled sand over the wet ink, rang the bell, and reached for the wax. When it was sealed I handed it to the lackey who had obeyed my summons. "Take this to Mr. Harry Sidney," I told him. "At once, please."

Lady Lucy and I had finished supper and were sitting in my withdrawing room later that day; she was sewing, and I was pretending to read. After a little while one of our house servants entered and announced that Harry Sidney and another gentleman were below and would like to see me.

I looked up and nodded. "I'm expecting them, Robert. Bring them to me here." Then, meeting Lady Lucy's questioning glance, I tried to reassure her. "Don't worry, cousin," I said. "This is something I feel I must do."

I had barely finished that last sentence when Harry came in, followed by Carl. Lady Lucy rose and dropped her needlework, her expression so much like that of a frightened rabbit that at any other time I might have been amused.

As she bowed and greeted them in a quavering voice I rose, too.

"Will you and Harry leave me with Carl for just a few minutes?" I said.

"If you wish," replied Harry. "But for only a few minutes, Lisa. Come, Lucy."

The moment we were alone, Carl, his blue eyes shining, sprang toward me. I stepped back, warding him off with my hands.

"No, no, Carl. Please!" Moving swiftly, I barricaded myself behind a tall carved chair, clinging to the back. "Please remain where you are. The others will return soon, and I must tell you why I asked Harry to bring you here tonight. You see, I was at the Old Bailey yesterday."

"So?" He smiled calmly and adjusted his lace cravat. "Then you know that my name is cleared. I'm glad you were there, my heart. It went well, I thought."

I stared at him and saw that he really meant what he was saying.

"It went well for you, perhaps," I replied slowly, "but what about the others? Your friend?"

He spread his hands wide and shrugged. "I know. It was most sad. If I could have helped them—but it was impossible. You were there, my Lisa. You must know that is true. They were careless, clumsy, I'm afraid." He shook his head, then smiled at me again. "So now we will forget all this. You are free. Now we think how to arrange our future."

For a moment I was speechless. "Future?" I asked, my voice rising. "We have no future, Carl! Do you think I'd marry a man who could let his friends and servants hang for carrying out his orders?" Gripping the chair back even more tightly, I forced myself to go on. "You may not consider yourself responsible for all these deaths, Carl, but I do. And I blame myself almost as much."

"But you wanted to be rid of Thynne, Lisa. You said you'd rather die than live with him!"

"I know," I answered sadly. "But not by murder."

While he still stood there, staring at me, I let go of the chair back and stepped toward him, holding out my hands, palms foremost. "You see, you've made me feel guilty of murder too. There's blood on my hands, Carl, and there's blood on yours. When the jury said 'not guilty' yesterday they were wrong. You *are* guilty and, because you did it for me, so am I."

His face was astonished and angry. Fortunately for me, Harry chose that moment to come back, moving swiftly to my side.

"With your permission, cousin, I'll say good night and take the Count with me. You have had a wearying, harrowing experience, and this must be the end of it."

I nodded in agreement. "Yes, as you say, Harry, this is the end of it. Farewell, my lord." I had turned to Carl, but I did not give him my hand. "For both our sakes, Carl, we will not meet again."

❧

Needless to say I slept little that night, and I woke the next morning feeling strangely languid. I tried to describe my unusual listlessness to Lady Temple, who came in to see me around midday.

"It's so odd," I told her. "I'm empty—remote. I'm away off somewhere."

"I know what you mean," Lady Temple replied. "I felt precisely that way after Diana died. It was like a blank lull, following a violent storm."

"Exactly. Did Harry tell you I asked him to bring Carl here to me last night?"

"Yes. He dropped in on his way home."

I picked up my needlework, looked at it blindly, and put it down. "Carl seemed to think that everything would be all right between us. He actually said we could now plan our future together! He—it was as if I were talking to a stranger; and when I told him that we were both guilty of murder, he stared at me with astonishment—astonishment and anger. Then, thank God, Harry came in and took him away. I was so exhausted I could hardly walk from here to my bedchamber!"

Before she could say anything, a lackey brought in a thick letter. "For you, milady," he said. "Milord is waiting for an answer."

I examined the coat of arms on the seal and the dashing foreign script that said "For the Lady Ogle." For a moment I was silent; then, putting it back on the servant's salver, I told him to take it away.

"Return it to Count von Königsmark," I said, "and tell him there is no answer. If he calls again, say I am not receiving visitors."

"I hope," said Lady Temple, after the servant had gone, "that you will still be firm when your numbness wears off. You are so tired now, Lisa, that you don't feel anything. It may be different later."

"Perhaps," I agreed, "but don't worry, dear lady. I won't see him again, no matter what happens. He was so callous during the trial." I shuddered, remembering it. "So—uncaring about his friend, Captain Vratz, and the others. It was as if he took a knife and cut my love for him right out of me. One moment I loved him; the next he was a stranger. How can that be?"

"It's because you loved your picture of him, Lisa, not

the man he really was. Your love disappeared as soon as you saw him clearly. This often happens, my child, especially when one is young and hungry for affection. Don't let it frighten you, or make you think you cannot love anyone else. Bitter as this experience has been, it will teach you to choose, next time, a man you can respect, a man who will be your friend as well as your lover."

She leaned over and kissed me fondly.

"Let's not talk about it any more. I really came to ask you what you plan to do. I don't think you should stay here; the word that you are in London has filtered around, and you may well be besieged by so-called friends who want to come and stare at the victim of the latest tragedy."

"I don't know," I said slowly. "I don't seem to care where I go or what I do." I tried to think, but it was no use. "I'll make up my mind after the hangings. Until then I'll stay in and refuse all visitors but you and Cousin Harry."

Lady Temple was with me again when Harry dropped in, a few days later. "I have letters for you, Lisa," he announced, "and some news. Which will you have first?"

Still tired and apathetic, I merely shrugged.

"If you had asked me," said Lady Temple, "I would have said the news."

"Well," replied Harry, sitting down, "I heard today that the Potter woman and her husband are suing Thynne's estate for five hundred pounds. They claim he promised to pay it to them within ten days after his marriage to you, Lisa, if they helped bring it about. They swear they did, which certainly proves our allegation that you were tricked and deceived."

"Then they are suing me, I suppose, as his widow. How

ironic to have to pay for being duped! Will we never reach the end of this business?"

"In time, my dear, in time. Which brings me to the other thing I have to tell you. You will be relieved to know that Königsmark has left England, probably forever. He's on his way to Venice to command a regiment under his famous Uncle Otto."

"Thank God!" said Lady Temple fervently. "I was afraid he might continue to make trouble for Lisa. He tried to see her again and sent several letters."

"What was in them, Lisa?"

"I sent them back unopened," I replied.

"Good girl. She's a very good girl, isn't she, Dorothy? Well, here are some letters you *will* want to open."

He handed me a little packet, and my two friends chatted softly together while I first read a long, rambling scribble from Princess Mary. I sighed, then tore open the other one and read it more hastily. I was still frowning when I put them down on the table. Lady Temple asked me what was wrong.

"Princess Mary wants me to come back to The Hague," I told her. "And she tells me her plan to rid herself of Betty Villiers went awry. Instead of taking Mary's letter to the Duke of York herself, she disobeyed Mary, sent it by messenger, stayed right at Harwich, and rushed back to Holland on the next packet boat. Now she's living privately with her sister Anne and some idiot was stupid enough to tell Mary that she slips into the Palace to see William after dark, hiding her face in a scarf."

"At least Mary doesn't have to suffer her presence in her household. Was William angry over the incident?"

"Apparently not. She writes they are good friends, these days. Perhaps he's tiring of that redheaded minx at last. I certainly hope so."

"And your other letter?"

"Oh," I answered hastily, "just a note. Charles Seymour would like to call, but I don't want any visitors but you two. I just want to be left alone!"

Captain Vratz and the other two men were hanged on the tenth day of March, but although I heard none of the details I could not stop myself from thinking about it during the long night hours, and by the end of the month I was in a very shaky condition.

"I'm going to talk to King Charles about you," said Lady Temple, one morning. "The Court comes back to Whitehall tomorrow, and I shall tell him you should leave London for a while. Perhaps he'll let me take you to Sheen. The weather will be turning warmer soon, you know, and the river is so beautiful in April. The willows all lacy and soft green, the birds courting, the baby lambs in the water meadows—"

For some strange reason I could not answer or listen to another word. Something seemed to snap inside me and I burst into violent tears, threw my needlework on the floor, and ran out of the room.

I don't know what Lady Temple said to the King, but I received a summons from him a few days later. He was alone in his presence chamber when I was ushered in, and he waited until I rose from my curtsy before greeting me.

"Come," he said gently, poking with a long finger at a footstool set near his throne chair. "Sit here where I can see you."

I obeyed him. He leaned forward, tipped up my face, and studied it intently.

"You've had a bad time, haven't you? That handsome

Swede of yours made a fine mess of things!"

To my horror I burst into tears and could not stop, just as I had done too many times recently.

"Here, here, this won't do!" protested the King. "I'm sorry, child. Forgive me! That was clumsy—stupid of me. Here, hold your old friend Frisky while I think this over."

Reaching down, he scooped up the sleeping spaniel and handed the soft little bundle to me, then sat back in his chair while I tried to regain my composure. Frisky snuggled into my arms and I buried my face in his silky fur. After the crying spell passed, I raised my eyes to his Majesty's long face.

"I'm the one to be sorry, sire," I said. Then, as the dog lapped at my chin with his wet tongue, I managed a watery smile. "He makes me realize how much I've been missing Whiskers. My cat," I explained hurriedly, as King Charles raised this thick eyebrows. "I haven't seen her since I was last at Petworth—a lifetime ago!"

"I know what you mean." He nodded understandingly. "A small animal can be a great comfort. I'm sure you'd give a great deal to have your Whiskers with you right now."

I agreed. "But I haven't heard from my grandmother since an angry, bitter letter I received in Holland about Mr. Thynne's murder, and no one at Petworth would have the authority to send my pet to me without her permission."

"In any case," said the King slowly, making a steeple of his fingers and placing them under his bony chin, "cats are happier at home. Perhaps you should go to Whiskers instead."

I stiffened. "Your Majesty!" I protested. "You wouldn't make me go back to my grandmother. Surely, you would not do that! I couldn't bear it!"

"No, no," he said hastily. "Not that, my dear. Not yet, anyway. She wants to make a tour of all the Percy houses, she tells me, as she does every year, beginning with Northumberland House and ending with Alnwick. So, as you prefer not to see her, I think you and Lady Lucy Hay might spend a few days at Sheen with the Temples, then, after Lady Percy leaves Petworth, go on down there and enjoy your own home and your pet."

While he was talking I was thinking of Petworth: my familiar rooms, the chapel, our comforting chaplain, the quiet. The gardens and the lake in April and May—

"Or would you rather return to The Hague?" asked the King.

I shook my head. "I don't feel well enough to be at Court, even with Princess Mary. But I'm afraid my grandmother will come back to Petworth and begin urging another marriage on me."

"That she will not do," promised King Charles firmly. "I'll settle that possibility right now."

Rising, he walked to a writing table and picked up his pen. "Greetings, et cetera," he read aloud as his hand moved swiftly over the paper. "I am sending Lady Ogle, in your absence, to recover her health and spirits at Petworth. She will continue to be under my personal protection as she has been for some months now, and I reiterate what I told you after Mr. Thynne's death—that any new plan for her future will be made by me at some later date, *if* it is made by anyone." He paused, looked over at me, and smiled.

"In the meantime she must have peace and quiet. When I go south during my summer's Progress, I shall make it a point to ride by Petworth to see that my orders have been carried out. By my own hand, this seventh day of April, in the year of Our Lord 1682. Charles Rex.

"There!" He threw down his pen and shook sand over the letter. "That, my dear child, should clip my lady's claws."

I was just about asleep when, as usual, a soft thump on the bed roused me. Smiling in the warm darkness, I reached down and drew my furry cat into the curve of my body. As Whiskers began to purr I snuggled deep into the pillows and realized that I was almost content. Not happy, of course, but content. And for the first time in so long that I could not count the months, I was sure I would sleep well.

Tomorrow should be pleasant, too; a quiet day. Every day now, for which I thanked God each night, was a quiet day. I had had weeks of them, and I no longer dreaded waking and facing the world.

I would spend as many hours as I wished in the garden, if the weather was fair, enjoying the sun and the flowers. And, at dinner and supper, I would eat what I wanted and chat easily with Lady Lucy.

My grandmother was still occupied elsewhere. I knew that she remained at Northumberland House, busy with

her card-playing friends, while the Court was at Westminster. Now she was probably on her way to Alnwick, but
she had been out of my life for so long that I barely
shivered at the thought of her return. King Charles had
finally made me realize that her power over me had been
limited.

Only once had I heard from her since coming here to
Petworth, a letter in which she told me I was a little fool
for refusing to see Charles Seymour when he had made a
special journey to Petworth to visit me. How she knew
about this I don't know; in any event, I did not answer it
or allow it to bother me.

I had my reasons for not seeing Charles, good reasons.
He must realize that I was not going to marry him or anyone else, and the sooner he forgot me the better for him.

But what a boy he had proven himself to be that day,
riding down in great state to court me! Lady Lucy, who had
received him and made my excuses, told me that he had
arrived with outriders, postilions, lackeys—and all wearing
fine velvet and silk liveries despite the hot June sun! Folly,
of course, to be formal with *me*, but sweet, amusing folly.

A few days after *that*, when I was in the garden cutting
a basketful of blossoms for my own apartments, I heard the
gate creak behind me; thinking it one of the gardeners, I
went on with my task, standing on tiptoe to clip off a
particularly beautiful deep red rose that swung almost out of
my reach.

A hand with a fall of rich lace on its wrist pulled it
down for me, and as I swung around, startled, I found myself, basket, scissors, and all, in Charles Seymour's arms.

Ducking my head away from his attempted kiss, I jerked
free and pointed the scissors at the middle of his hand-
somely embroidered waistcoat.

"Charles!" I protested. "Behave yourself!" Then, real-

izing suddenly how ridiculous I must look, fending him
off with the garden shears, I burst out laughing. After a
moment he joined in, and we simply stood there in the
sunny, fragrant enclosure, laughing together.

He made another dart at me but I stepped back, my
ludicrous weapon ready, and again we laughed. I sobered
first; I put down the basket and scissors and nodded to a
stone bench.

"Come and sit down while I scold you, Charles. You
know perfectly well I prefer not to see you these days—or
anyone."

When he opened his mouth to protest, I silenced him.
"No, let me finish. It's unfair of you to force yourself on
me this way; you merely make it difficult for us both. Now
I have to say what would be better unsaid, that I want you
to forget all about me. I like you too much to want to hurt
you, but I am not ever going to marry again—not you or
anyone else."

Again he tried to speak and again I refused to listen.
"Surely you understand how I feel?" I asked, my voice
breaking. "One man shot because of me, and three hanged.
And all because Carl and I fell in love and wanted to
marry!"

"Of course I understand, Lisa. But no matter what you
think, it was *not* your fault. Not in any way. And you cannot waste the rest of your life because of what someone
else did. What good would it do?"

"I didn't say it would do any good. That's not the point."
I paused and tried to find the right words. "I feel there's
a curse on me, Charles. I seem to bring death to the men
I marry and disaster and difficulties to those I love. So
please do as I ask. Go away and forget me."

Charles shook his head, drew me close to his side, and
dropped a kiss on the top of my head.

"Foolish Lisa! As if I'd be frightened away by your curse, as you call it. That's all nonsense. You've been the victim of unscrupulous people, determined to have their way regardless of how it affects you. But it's over now and it can't happen again; the King will see to that. So stop fretting and let yourself be happy."

"I can't. It's not that easy. No, don't argue any more, Charles. If you care for me even a little, go away and find someone else."

"I'll go, but I won't forget you or find anyone else. And I will come back, no matter what you say." He rose and looked down at me. "I'll be back—and soon."

❧

As the June days wore on, each lovelier than the last, I found myself remembering the young Duke's promise to return. He had said *soon*, but he didn't appear and there was no news of him. Perhaps, I told myself, my words had taken effect after all. Perhaps he had decided I was right and had turned his attention elsewhere.

This thought, which should have made me relieved and happy, was rather depressing, and I scolded myself for such weakness and vanity. Was I one of those dreadful women who enjoyed keeping men dangling after them?

As I asked the question I strayed to the window and looked up the road that passed our gates. Except for the innkeeper's dog, scratching a flea, it was empty. I sighed. I was lonely, that was the trouble. Those busy days in Holland had spoiled me—the dancing and skating, the trip to Amsterdam with Mary, her understanding and companionship, our long talks—

I shook myself angrily. What nonsense! Here I was at Petworth, where I wanted to be, safe, quiet, away from the world and its problems, no longer at my grandmother's mercy. What more could I ask? This was my life and would be from now on; I should be grateful for it. Grateful and content. Why on earth not?

✧

July brought a great deal of rain, and, probably because I was forced to remain indoors, I grew increasingly restless. I passed many an afternoon writing long letters to Princess Mary and Lady Temple; I walked up and down the Long Gallery with Lady Lucy; I sewed and read. This, of course, was the usual life for a spinister, and I often looked at Lady Lucy, thinking of the years ahead, and wondered.

Then, toward the end of the month, the weather changed for the better and we had a whole week of glorious sunny days. I stood, one warm afternoon, in the small salon that overlooked a wide spread of velvet lawn and our pretty lake beyond. Should I wander out and feed the spotted deer cropping the grass nearby, or should I call for my groom and little white mare and ride for an hour or two?

The cloudless blue sky, the soft breeze riffling the willow fronds at the water's edge, the cheerful voices of the gardeners working out of sight of the windows, all told me this day was too fine to be wasted.

I had decided on the ride when the chamberlain entered, his face an odd mixture of awe and excitement.

"My lady," he said, gulping a bit, "it's the King! He just rode into the courtyard like—like anyone else! 'I want to see Lady Ogle,' he told me, and sat down in that big chair in the hall. Should I fetch Lady Lucy, or bring him to you?"

"I'll go—no, bring him here to me, please," I replied, as startled as the man himself. "And see that we have wine, fruit, cakes. Hurry! We mustn't keep him waiting."

Almost before I had time to glance in the looking glass
and tuck up a loose red curl, the door opened again.

"His Majesty, my lady."

"Sire!" I dipped to the floor as King Charles strode to
my side.

"My lady Ogle." Raising me, he kissed me on the cheek,
turned me so that the light from the windows fell on my
face, and smiled.

"Well, you look quite your lovely self again, my dear. I
see that my medicine has done its work."

I dropped my eyes, feeling shy, and thanked him. Should
I send for Lady Lucy Hay, I asked him, and would he
honor us by staying for supper?

"My business is with you, my child. We need not disturb
Lady Lucy. And although I would like nothing better than
to sup with you, my good friend Montagu expects me back
at Cowdray before long. It's only a few miles, you know."

A lackey, almost falling over his feet as he stared at the
King, set a tray down on a table.

I dismissed him. "I would like to serve you myself, sire,
if you will allow me the privilege."

"A glass of wine, then, but nothing else. Our friends feed
us only too well when we travel around the country." He
waited until he had sipped half of the hippocras I poured
into our best crystal goblet, then sat down rather abruptly
in a chair beside one of the windows.

"Come here, Lisa, and let me talk to you."

Feeling more than a little frightened, I obeyed him.
What was his business with me today? My heart sank, remembering his letter to my grandmother.

"I believe it has been almost a half year since Thomas
Thynne was killed. Am I right?" He counted the months
off on his long fingers. "February, March, April, May, June,
July—long enough, certainly, for you to remain in seclu-

sion. Even our most stiff-necked friends would agree that the word mourning would be ridiculous in your case."

As he spoke, he leaned forward and studied my face.

"The important thing, however, is that you have regained your health and, with it, your peace of mind. If so, we must begin to consider your future. I don't want to hurry you, my child, but I warn you that Lady Percy is growing a bit restive; she has written me several times recently, saying that if I have no plans for you she will be happy to find you another suitable husband."

"*Another* suitable husband?" I repeated the phrase grimly "I hope, sire, you do not agree with her ideas of who is suitable!"

"Hardly." He laughed. "But although I have not yet told her so, it happens that I *do* have a plan for this little hand." He took my fingers in his and spread them apart. "I would like, with your permission, to bestow it on someone *I* consider suitable. He's rather young, perhaps, but he's of good blood, has a fine fortune, and should make you very happy."

My heart sank lower with every word. Young, good blood, a fine fortune, indeed! So he was still determined to have me for that nine-year-old son of his. What a fool I had been to think King Charles my friend; his purpose, always, had been to arrange another dreadful marriage for me—one *he* wanted!

A sob rose in my throat and I turned my head away. The hand holding mine tightened and King Charles rose from his seat, placed his other arm around my waist, and drew me gently but firmly to the window.

"As a matter of fact," he said gravely, "I brought the young man with me today. Look, there he is."

Was there to be no end to this torment? Tears misted my eyes when I tried to obey. Standing on the terrace below us was a tall, slender man, his face hidden under a wide hat loaded with beautiful plumes; as I stared, blinking my eyes to clear them, I saw Whiskers stroll around the corner of the house and approach him.

He bent over and, as she stopped at his feet and sat down, he reached out a hand and rubbed her behind the ears and under the chin. A moment later, to my great astonishment, Whiskers flopped flat on her back, her plump white stomach exposed, her four paws in the air, inviting him to tickle her furry belly.

"And that, I suppose," said King Charles, "is your cat Whiskers. My friend has a way with cats, doesn't he? I like that, don't you? A 'gentle man' in the best sense of the word. Ah—"

The stranger, apparently sensing that someone was watching him, raised his head and looked up at the window.

I stared in disbelief. "Why, it's Charles Seymour!" I said slowly. "It—it's Charles!"

The King's long arm drew me closer. He laughed softly. "Is there any reason why it shouldn't be Charles?"

He looked inquiringly at me, but I could think of nothing to say.

"As it happens, I think it should be, and so do your other good friends. Lady Temple, Harry Sidney, my niece Mary —they have all told me that you and the Duke of Somerset would be well matched and that you are not completely indifferent to him. Of course, they may be quite wrong."

Again he looked at me with his brows raised; again I could think of nothing to say. My head was whirling, my thoughts a mass of confusion.

"Then allow me to ask you another question. But I want the truth, child, so listen carefully: If I should say to you today, 'I, Charles Rex, command you, Elizabeth, Lady

Ogle, to wed Charles Seymour, the Duke of Somerset,' what would you reply?"

I could feel the hot, telltale color come and go in my cheeks, and for a long minute the room was absolutely quiet. Then I heard a clock strike and Charles, on the terrace, laughing at Whiskers.

I raised my head and my eyes met the King's black ones. They were twinkling at me so merrily that I gave a little chuckle.

"Well, your Majesty," I replied demurely, "if I must really answer truthfully, I would assure you that I am, as I always am, your most obedient servant!"

❧

The night before my third wedding I lay awake, thinking of all the reasons I had given Charles for not ever marrying again. I had almost forgotten them during the intervening days; now they returned to haunt me.

I tossed and turned for hours, before finally falling asleep. But in my dreams, I found myself on the way to the altar, walking slowly beside King Charles who was to give me away.

Everything was as it should be; I was clad in my ravishing silver brocade gown, my well-brushed hair was hanging to my waist, and all my friends were there, smiling at me as we passed up the aisle.

Then I saw who was waiting beside the chaplain and I halted abruptly. How could they smile when that horrible little Harry Ogle was to be my bridegroom? No, no, it wasn't Harry, it was Thomas Thynne! I tried to tell the King, to protest, but the words wouldn't come out. He was smiling, too!

Now we were closer to the altar and my eyes met those of the man standing there. Mother of God, it wasn't

Thomas Thynne any more, it was Carl! No, no, I couldn't
—I wouldn't.

As I struggled I half roused, and a great warm golden
flood of relief and happiness swept over me. It wasn't
Henry Ogle or Thomas Thynne or Carl—

It was Charles. "I'm marrying Charles," I told myself.
"I'm awake, and this is my real wedding day at last. I'm
going to be happy—because I'm marrying *Charles!*"